Then he moved quicker than she'd anticipated, and before she could stop him, he'd wrapped his arms around her waist and pushed her back against the wall.

"What if I said I want you?" he asked, his breath fanning warmly over her face.

"For…for Christmas?" she asked, and felt like a colossal idiot.

He didn't smile, but shook his head, his hands slipping under her coat to rub along her back. "No. Right now. I want you, Morgan."

He moved again and Morgan saw his arm lifting. He was going to touch her. No, wait, he was already touching her. She should move. She should put lots of distance between them to keep whatever was about to happen from happening. But she didn't. She couldn't. His fingers grazed her jaw, came over her chin, then up to tap her bottom lip.

"You can't want me," she said, her body beginning to tremble even though it was the last thing she wanted to do.

Dear Reader,

I love writing Christmas stories!

With that said, I was more than excited to begin the new Taylors of Temptation series with a Christmas-themed book. Gray and Morgan were the perfect couple to start with, as they were both struggling with things that distracted them from the holidays.

The Taylor sextuplets were born in Temptation, Virginia—a small town that I created because I like the community and closeness of small-town stories. The sextuplets were taken away from their hometown at a young age, now they've all come back, some to stay, and some just to visit. But when they return, they'll remember all the magic that was once there.

When Gray returned to Temptation, he was certain that it would be temporarily, until he met Morgan and her twins. Their love wasn't instant, but that initial incessant pull that refuses to let go when a couple first meets was definitely present. Unraveling all the layers of Gray's past feelings and Morgan's past losses was a task. Thankfully, I had lots of Christmas music and movies to help me along the way!

I hope you enjoy this first glimpse at the Taylors and have fun spending the holidays in Temptation!

Happy reading,

A.C. Arthur

One Mistletoe Wish

A.C. Arthur

HARLEQUIN® KIMANI™ ROMANCE

Recycling programs
for this product may
not exist in your area.

ISBN-13: 978-0-373-86477-5

One Mistletoe Wish

For questions and comments about the quality of this book please contact us
at CustomerService@Harlequin.com.

H HARLEQUIN®
www.Harlequin.com

Printed in U.S.A.

A.C. Arthur was born and raised in Baltimore, Maryland, where she currently resides with her husband and three children. An active imagination and a love for reading encouraged her to begin writing in high school, and she hasn't stopped since.

Working in the legal field for almost thirteen years, she's seen lots of horrific things and longs for the safe haven reading a romance novel brings. Determined to bring a new edge to romance, she continues to develop intriguing plots, sensual love scenes, racy characters and fresh dialogue—thus keeping readers on their toes!

For all the latest news on A.C. Arthur's books, giveaways, appearances and discussions, join A.C.'s Book Lounge on Facebook at Facebook.com/pages/AC-Arthurs-Book-Lounge/140199625996114.

Books by A.C. Arthur

Harlequin Kimani Romance

Defying Desire
Full House Seduction
Summer Heat
Sing Your Pleasure
Touch of Fate
Winter Kisses
Desire a Donovan
Surrender to a Donovan
Decadent Dreams
Eve of Passion
One Mistletoe Wish

Visit the Author Profile page at
Harlequin.com for more titles.

To those who watch Christmas movies
and listen to Christmas music all year long. You rock!

Chapter 1

"Bah, hamburger!" Ethan Malloy shouted. His skinny arms were wrapped around his chest, lips poked out and still red from the punch he'd had during the break.

Morgan Hill rubbed her temples and held back a sigh.

"It's humbug, Ethan. Say it slower this time and remember the word is *humbug*."

He wouldn't remember. Or rather, he did know the correct pronunciation, but Ethan thought he was a five-year-old Kevin Hart, minus the cursing. So everything he said or did was in search of a chuckle or a laugh from those around him—his audience, so to speak. His personality worked Morgan's last nerve. She'd chastised herself more than once about feeling this way about a little boy. She was trained to deal with children, as she'd gone to the University of Maryland and received her bachelor's degree in elementary education. Unfortunately, there were no classes that would have prepared her for Ethan Malloy.

He was the only child of Rayford Malloy, the sixty-three-year-old president of the Temptation town council, and Ivonne Danner-Malloy, his twenty-five-year-old video-dance-queen wife. Between his father being too busy and too tired to discipline him and his mother being too young, too conceited and too everything else to be bothered, Ethan never had a chance. Those were the reasons Morgan used a good portion of her patience with the child. Morgan's granny always said—whenever Ida Mae Bonet had the displeasure of being in the presence of her brother's children—"we don't get to choose who our parents are."

That was certainly the truth, Morgan thought as she watched Ethan continue with his rendition of the scene where Ebenezer Scrooge continued to refuse heat or any other comfort for his only employee, Bob Cratchit, played by seven-year-old Wesley Walker. Wesley, unlike Ethan, knew his lines and probably the lines of everyone else in the play. He was a perfectionist and determined to prove himself to everyone in this small town, despite the fact that his father had run off and left his mother with four kids, a broken-down old Nissan and a mountain of debt. It was a shame, Morgan thought as she watched the young fella on stage, walking around and holding his head up high— even though Bob Cratchit wasn't such a proud man. But a boy at such a tender age shouldn't be faced with the gossip and cruelty that could be dished out in a small town.

They lived in Temptation, Virginia, population 14,364 as of the last census, two years ago. Temptation had a rich history and struggled to catch up with the modern world. With its ten-member town council—the majority of whom were descendants from families that had been around since the town's inception in the 1800s—and the newly elected mayor, Cinda Pullum, going toe-to-toe in battles over everything from revitalizing Mountainview Park to the weekly trash pickup, Temptation could be as lively as any of the reality shows that littered today's television channels.

The town could also be as traditional and heartwarming as an old black-and-white movie with things such as the annual Christmas Eve celebration, which included the play that Morgan and her crew of youngsters were now painstakingly rehearsing. There were two things Morgan loved about living in Temptation—the traditions and the resilience of the citizens. No matter what the people of this town had gone through—from the Civil War to the dark days of the Great Depression and the hostile times of the Civil Rights movement—they'd always bounced back and they never stopped doing the things that made the town so special in the first place. The families were the heart of Temptation, as they were determined to live in harmony in their little part of the world. More recent and localized catastrophes had hit Temptation and now, sadly, Morgan found herself living through her own test as a citizen of the town.

"You should put him out, Mama."

The soft voice of Morgan's five-year-old daughter, Lily, interrupted her thoughts.

"What?" Morgan asked.

Lily looked up from where she was sitting cross-legged on the floor with an unruly stack of twinkle lights in her lap. Her little hands had been moving over the strands in an attempt to separate the tangled mass for the last half hour. There hadn't been much progress but Lily was much more patient than Morgan would ever claim to be. She was also the prettiest little girl Morgan had seen in all her twenty-eight years.

Her daughter shook her head, two long ponytails swaying with the motion.

"He's a mess," she told Morgan. "A hot mess, like Aunt Wendy says all the time."

Morgan couldn't help it, she smiled. Wendy, her older sister by barely a year, talked a mile a minute and Lily always seemed to be around soaking up each and every word that fell out of Wendy's mouth, good or bad.

"He's trying," Morgan told her, knowing without any doubt who her daughter thought was a hot mess. "We have to give him a chance."

Lily shook her head again. "No, we don't. You're in charge."

She was, Morgan thought, even if she didn't feel that way. She hadn't wanted Ethan for the lead in the play in the first place. But Rayford had stopped by her house the Monday before Thanksgiving and told her in no uncertain terms that he expected his "boy" to have a prominent part in the play this year. Especially since this was most likely the last year the community center would be open to house the play and the Christmas celebration. Morgan and a good majority of the town had been worried about this hundred-year-old building and two others—the Plympton House, which had been converted into a hospital during the war, then restored, expanded and renamed All Saints Hospital in the sixties, and the Taylor House, a now almost dilapidated Victorian that had once been the home of the town's biggest financial benefactor. She'd been so concerned with the possible loss of three of the town's historic buildings that she hadn't had the energy to fight with Rayford about something as trivial as his son's part in a play. Now, however, she wished she'd mustered up some resistance because Lily was right, Ethan was a hot mess.

"I wanna load the presents," another child's voice called from behind Morgan and before she could move a hand, there was tugging on the hem of her shirt.

"Didn't you say it was my turn to load the presents in the sleigh, Mama? You told me last night, 'cause I'm tall enough to do it."

Morgan turned around ready to reply to her son with his dark brown eyes—slanted slightly in the corners as a result of his father's half Korean, half African American heritage—and butter-toned complexion, courtesy of Morgan's mother and grandmother, who were descendants of the Creole-born Bonets of Louisiana. His twin sister had the same features. Jack and Lily were different, not only by their gender, but they also had opposite personalities. Where Lily was quiet and somewhat serious, Jack was boisterous and playful. They were sometimes like night and day, but always the very best of Morgan and her late husband, James. Each day she looked into their precious little faces she was reminded of that fact and, at the same time, overwhelmed with love and grief.

James Stuart Hill had been a wonderful man. Kind, loving, compassionate and totally committed to his young wife and family. Morgan had met him in Baltimore, during her senior year of college. He'd been on leave from the army to finalize the sale of his late mother's convenience store and her house. An American-born Korean, Mary Kim had raised her only child alone, after his African American father had been shot to death in an attempted robbery. Although Morgan had never met Mary, she felt she'd known the woman through the great man she'd raised.

Their courtship had been fast and passionate and by the time Morgan graduated from college, she'd learned that she was pregnant. James was leaving for a year-long tour in Hawaii two weeks later. So they married quickly in Granny's backyard and then traveled to Honolulu, where she gave birth to her two precious jewels. A year later James received a temporary assignment in Virginia and Morgan came home to Temptation with her twins, where the four of them had lived a happy, normal life. Until James was shipped off to Afghanistan. He was killed a week before the twins' second birthday. Three years later, the pain of that day still had the power to take Morgan's breath away.

"Some people are only in your life for a season," Granny had said as she'd stood leaning on her cane.

They'd been at the cemetery then, the one in Maryland right next to where James had buried his mother. Hours later they were back in Temptation and Morgan was tasked with raising her two young children alone. With the love and support from her grandmother and her sister, she'd managed to make it through those first tough weeks. She'd taken a job as a first-grade teacher at the elementary school, went to church on Sundays and played all day with her babies on Saturdays. Her life had managed to move on even though there were still some days when all she wanted to do was cry for all the possibilities that had been lost.

"Marley's coming! Marley's coming!" Alana, a six-year-old playing one of Bob Cratchit's children, yelled from where she was sitting at the end of the stage.

"It's not time yet," Ethan complained. "I'm not finished saying 'bah, hamburger.'"

"He needs to shut up," Lily said with a sigh.

"You're not adding the chains this time, Mama," Jack stated loudly. As if the noisier he said it, the faster she would start doing it.

Usually, when it was time for Jacob Marley—played by Malcolm Washington, who was missing one of his front teeth—to make his ghostly appearance, Wendy, who was her part-time assistant whenever she wasn't on duty at the hospital, would knock on the desk to make the footstep sounds and rattle the bike chains in her bag. But Ethan was right, it wasn't time for Jacob's appearance quite yet.

Still, Morgan could not deny the sound of footsteps coming fast and almost furiously down the hallway toward the hall where they were rehearsing.

"Hush, children," she said as she stood.

Morgan was walking toward the door, or rather tiptoeing like she actually expected to see the ghost of Jacob Marley come through that doorway, just like she knew the now-quiet children were. The footsteps continued and so did Morgan. She was wearing her bright orange-and-fuchsia tennis shoes today, along with her black running suit, which Wendy said made her look more like a teenage track star than a grown woman. Morgan tended to ignore her older sister when it came to dressing because Wendy was a proud member of the single, sexy and seriously looking club. Whereas Morgan was a mother and a teacher and she was perfectly content with that.

"Oh!" she yelled.

"Sorry," a voice said as he reached out to grab her shoulders and keep her upright.

She'd bumped into what felt like a concrete wall and was embarrassed to discover it was simply a man's chest. Well, there was really nothing simple about this man or his chest, which she figured out the moment she stepped back and looked up at him.

He was tall with a honey-brown complexion, a strong jaw, a precisely cut goatee and seductive dark brown eyes. His shoulders were broad, the suit he wore expertly cut. His hair was wavy and black, his lips of medium thickness.

Morgan almost sighed. If this was the ghost of Jacob Marley, then she was seriously going to consider crossing over to the land of the walking dead, because standing before her was one fine-ass black man.

Gray removed his hands from her instantly. He had no choice. The warmth that had immediately spread up his arms and to his chest was so intense he thought of the heart attack that had killed his father two months ago. Sure, Gray visited his internist once a year for a physical, so he knew that he was in perfect health, but the feeling had shocked him.

She had shocked him.

"Are you all right?" he asked. She'd taken a step back from him, looking as if she'd seen a ghost.

A number of children had almost instantly flocked around her, as if offering their juvenile protection, should he be there for some nefarious reason. He wasn't, or at least he didn't think of it that way. Still, they were all glaring at him. Something else that made Gray uncomfortable.

"I'm fine," she answered, clearing her throat. "Can I help you with something?"

Gray didn't need anyone's help. He hadn't for a very long time, but that was not his response. At thirty years old, Gray had been running his own company for fifteen years, supervising billion-dollar deals and working with brilliant tech minds to create the most innovative products in the world. He could certainly travel back to the small, dilapidated town that had torn his family apart and take care of the sale of three measly buildings without anyone's help. Hence the reason he had secured a limited power-of-attorney document from each of his siblings. There was no need for all of them to come back to the place they all hated. He was the oldest and, as usual, he'd decided to bear the brunt of an unpleasant task.

"My name is Grayson Taylor," he told her. "I own this building."

"Oh," she'd said, taking another step back as if she was afraid he'd reach out and touch her again.

Gray frowned.

"I'm just stopping by to take a look around as I'll be selling the building hopefully in the next couple of months."

"Christmas is next month," the little girl holding tightly to the woman's hand told him matter-of-factly.

He nodded. "Yes. It is."

She was a cute little girl, with an intense stare that shouldn't have unnerved him, but just like touching the woman had, it did.

"Even though the sales probably won't be official until after the first of the year, I need to do a walk-through before then. I'll send my lawyers a report and they'll get started with the listing. If you don't mind, could you show me around?" he asked, returning his gaze to the woman.

His question was met with immediate silence and after a few seconds she shook her head. "I'm rehearsing with the children. We're just getting started with regularly scheduled rehearsals and the play is in four weeks. They have school during the day. We only have the weekends and an hour and a half in the evenings to rehearse."

Gray presumed she was telling him "no." That wasn't a word women usually used with him, but his ego wasn't bruised. This was business after all.

"Fine. I'll wait until the rehearsal is finished," he said. "Can I sit over here?"

There were chairs scattered about the spacious room, some lined directly in front of the small stage, where he suspected they were rehearsing their little play.

"You can watch me be Scrooge," a boy wearing a frizzy white wig and an oversize black tuxedo jacket with tails told him.

He'd stepped away from the woman and her entourage and motioned for Gray to follow him. Admiring the child's initiative, Gray walked behind him, leaving the still-leery gaze of the woman behind.

She didn't say another word, but moved across the room and gave instructions for the children to resume their places and continue. The little girl who had been holding her hand still stood right beside her, but the child peeked back at Gray more than once. She had questions, he thought. Who was he? Why was he here and what did that possibly mean for them? He'd stared into her pensive eyes and felt the urge to answer all her questions in a way that would make her stop looking at him with such sincere inquisitiveness. It was the strangest thought he'd ever had, especially since Gray wasn't known to get caught up in anyone's emotions about anything.

He was the strongest of the Taylor sextuplets, the first one to be born on that humid July evening thirty years ago. His brothers and sisters all shared his birthday, but none of them had ever shared the weight of being the first baby born of the first set of multiples in the town of Temptation. That had been his title for the first seven years of his life—"the first born of the first Temptation sextuplets." *The Taylors of Temptation* was what they'd named the reality show that featured his parents as they brought home their six bundles of joy and lived in the huge blue-and-white Victorian with the river at its back. As Gray recalled, the show would have been more aptly named if it had been called *Terror of the Taylors* instead.

"Do you like Christmas?"

He was yanked from his thoughts by the soft voice of the little girl who had been sneaking glances at him. Her hair was dark and long, brushing past her shoulders with red bows at the end of each ponytail. She wore jeans and a red-and-white striped sweater. Her boots had black-and-white polka dots.

"I don't know," he replied. "Do you like Christmas?"

She nodded and said, "Yes. I do. So does my mother."

As she said those words Gray nodded. "Is your mother up there directing the play?"

"Yes. Her name is Morgan Hill. She's a teacher, too."

"You're not supposed to talk to strangers," a little boy said as he came up beside the girl and pulled on her arm.

She jerked away. "He's not a stranger. His name is Grayson Taylor and he owns this building."

Gray didn't like the stoic way in which she'd mimicked his previous words.

"We don't know him, so he's a stranger," the boy, who looked a little like the girl, said. "I'm gonna tell Mama."

Gray almost smiled, but he felt his forehead drawing into a frown instead. Twins?

"No need to tell," he declared. "How about we all go up front and sit with your mother? That way she'll know where you both are."

It would also give Gray a chance to ask a few questions about the building. From the looks of the outside, he didn't think he'd get much for the building itself, but the land might be worth something. Between the sale of this building, the hospital and the house, the total should be a good chunk to split between the six of them. Not that Gray needed the money. His vision and the talented people he'd hired to work at Gray Technologies had made him a rich man years ago. No, any money that came from the properties would be what the Taylor sextuplets thought of as their father's payment for destroying their lives all those years ago.

"Mama, he wants to sit with you," the little girl said when they'd come to a stop next to the chair where her mother sat.

Morgan looked up from her clipboard and then hastily stood. "Oh, I apologize," she said. "I hope they weren't bothering you."

Now it was Gray's turn to simply stare. She was very pretty, he thought, as if he hadn't noticed that before. Her skin was smooth and unmarred by any cosmetics. Gray was used to seeing more glamorous women, from the ones he worked with to the ones trying to get into his bed. High heels, tight dresses, heavily made-up faces and beaming smiles—that's what he was used to.

Morgan was looking at him like she couldn't decide

whether to curse him out or be cordial to him. The look, coupled with the stubborn lift of her chin and the set of her shoulders, tugged at something deep inside him. Glancing away was not an option.

"He doesn't know if he likes Christmas, Mama," the little girl said.

"She's always telling," the boy added with a shake of his head.

"Hush," Morgan told them.

"Ms. Hill! Ms. Hill! Ethan forgot what to say," another child's voice exclaimed.

"I did not! I'm imposizing. That's what actors do," the boy in the white wig—who Gray now knew was named Ethan—argued.

"The word is *improvising*, Ethan, and I'd prefer if you just repeated what's written in the script," Morgan replied.

She'd moved quickly, heading to the stage where the two arguing children stood. She spoke in a voice that was much calmer than he suspected she was feeling. She guided the children to where she wanted them to stand on the stage and spoke the lines she wanted them to repeat, all while Ethan looked as if he had other, more exciting things to do.

"He thinks he knows everything," the little girl told Gray.

She'd scooted onto one of the chairs by then.

"Be quiet, Lily. Mama's gonna show Ethan who's the boss," the boy told her.

"I think he's the boss," Lily said to her brother and they both looked up to Gray.

He was just about to speak—to say what, Gray wasn't totally sure—when the lights suddenly went out. Screams were immediate and should have been expected since Gray didn't think there was anyone in this room over the age of six or seven, besides him and Morgan.

"Stay calm," he heard Morgan say over the growing

chaos of children's voices. "It's probably just a blown fuse again. I'll take care of it."

Gray slipped his phone from his jacket pocket and turned on the flashlight app, but when he attempted to take a step toward the stage, he found his moves hampered. Gray was six-two and he weighed two hundred and thirty-five pounds, which consisted of mostly muscle thanks to the ten to twelve hours a week he spent at the gym. Last year he'd run in the 5K marathon to fight diabetes and finished in under fifteen minutes, so there should have been no problem with him walking across this room to assist Morgan in whatever was going on. Except for the two sets of arms that had wrapped tightly around each of his thighs, holding him down like weights.

Chapter 2

"Here's the fuse box," Morgan stated about two seconds before Gray's hands brushed over hers.

"I'll take care of it," he said, moving her hand to the side.

"You don't know anything about this building," she snapped. Her hand was still warm from where he'd touched her and Morgan rubbed it against her thigh as if she thought that would erase her reaction to his touch.

He was holding his phone, with its glaring light, pointed toward the fuse box, but Morgan could see the shadow of his face as he turned to look at her.

"I own this building," he replied.

Morgan huffed. "That doesn't mean you know your way around it, or how much it means to the people of this town," she quipped.

It was really hot in here. They were in the basement and Morgan tried to take a step back, but there was only a wall behind her. To her right was a door that led to the crawl space. To her left, the wall with the fuse box. Directly in front of her, the man with the flashlight and delicious-smelling cologne.

"But I do know how to turn on," he began, still watching her and, if she wasn't mistaken, moving a step closer.

Morgan tried to shift to the side, but she stumbled on some cords that were lying on the floor and ended up against his chest, again. The light from the phone wavered as his hands dropped to her shoulders, sliding down slowly as he kept her from falling. Embarrassed and irritated by the heat that had spread quickly from the hand that he'd touched moments ago to the rest of her body, Morgan tried to pull away from him. She slammed her back into the wall.

He shone the light in her face at that point, then looked at her as if he was going to…no, he wasn't, Morgan thought quickly. He wouldn't dare.

"It's the last circuit breaker," she said, hastily pointing over his shoulder. "That's the one that usually blows. It's been doing that for the past couple of months. Harry said he was going to look at it, but he hasn't had a chance."

Harry Reed owned the hardware store and worked part-time at his family's B and B. He also did handiwork around the town in his spare time, for which Morgan knew a lot of people were very grateful.

Now Grayson looked confused, which was just fine because that's exactly how Morgan was feeling.

"You just open the box and—"

He backed away from her and said, "I know how to flip the circuit breakers and turn on the lights."

The phone's flashlight moved and she could see him opening the box now.

"You're right," he told her as he began flipping the first breaker off and then on. "I don't know about this building, but I do know about fuse boxes. Turn everything off and hopefully, when you turn it back on…" He let his voice trail off as that last fuse clicked off and then…

"All power is restored," he said the moment the tight hallway they'd been standing in was once again illuminated.

Behind him, the kids who they couldn't leave in the dark room alone cheered.

"Great," Morgan replied. "Thank you."

She let out a whoosh of breath as she hurriedly slipped past him. It was a weird move, she knew, as she flattened against one wall and shimmied around the spot where he still stood, but Morgan didn't care. She simply needed to get out of that corner with him.

"That was fun," Ethan said immediately as she approached. "Can we do it again?"

"I'm hungry, Ms. Hill," Daisy Lynn added with a baleful look.

Morgan had a headache.

She looked at her watch and let out a sigh. "It's almost time for your parents to pick you up anyway. So let's get back upstairs and clean up our props. We'll rehearse again tomorrow after Sunday services," she told them.

She led the group up the basement steps and through the double doors. When they'd come down moments ago Morgan had instructed them to hold hands and onto the railing. This time, since the lights were on and probably because Morgan's thoughts were somewhere else, she hadn't instructed them to do the same. The lights were brighter in the upstairs hallways and the children ran to the main hall, where they'd been rehearsing. She was walking and thinking about him, but somehow completely forgetting that she'd left Grayson Taylor down in the basement.

"Considering running away before giving me the tour of the place?" he said from behind her.

"What?" Morgan said as she spun around to face him.

Her feet almost twisted as she did, but luckily she was able to right herself. Why had she become so clumsy around this man? "I'm not running anywhere. I have to tend to the children first," she told him.

He nodded, but didn't seem to believe her. That irritated Morgan and her headache throbbed more insistently.

"Look," she said with a sigh, "I may not be the right person to give you this tour. I'm pretty attached to this building. And to the hospital, since I was born there. That means I'm going to be pretty irritated when you knock down the buildings or sell them off to some developer who'll knock them down to build a strip mall or some other big-city franchise that we don't need around here."

Damn. She hadn't meant to say all that, at least not to his face. He slipped his hands into the front pockets of his pants and watched as she wondered what to say next. Nothing about her personal feelings, she decided. Temptation was her home. These buildings, the landmarks and the people all meant something to her. She understood that it would be difficult for outsiders to understand that connection, but Grayson Taylor wasn't an outsider. At least, he shouldn't have been.

"Millie Randall works with the chamber of commerce. Her office is in city hall. She'll be the better person to show you around. They open Monday at nine," she said with finality and turned to walk away.

"It's not my intention to knock anything down," he told her. "I plan for a quick sale."

"That's your business, Mr. Taylor," she replied without turning to face him.

"I'm not your enemy," he said when he'd easily caught up with her.

"And you're not a friend," she replied. "Now, if you'll excuse me, I have to go."

She did have to go. The children were waiting for her.

Their parents would arrive soon and she needed to clean up the hall and then get Lily and Jack home to feed them dinner. She did not have time to hang around at the community center with the man who could single-handedly take the building away from them. She definitely did not have to like how he looked and smelled, and damn, how it felt whenever he touched her. No, she didn't and wouldn't like any of that. Morgan promised herself she would not.

Gray ran fast and hard across the field of crisp frost-tipped grass. The air was cool and the sky a dull gray. The scents of nearby animals and the sounds of early-morning farm life wafted all around. This wasn't the NordicTrack he used in his home gym, or the three-mile track that looped around the top level of the condo building where he lived. Gray ran on either of those on a daily basis. When he was out of town on business, the five-star hotels where he stayed always had state-of-the-art gyms with top-of-the-line equipment, including pools where he could indulge in slow leisurely laps to relax his muscles after a hard workout.

The brochure on the table in the room had called it the Owner's Suite, but to him, it looked like a top floor had been added to an old horse's stable.

Gray had been out for more than an hour and he was sure he'd run well over five miles by now and seen more grassy hills and fog-covered mountaintops than he had in all his life. It would have been a breathtaking view for someone who didn't prefer the city life of bright lights, fast cars and hot women.

The latter, Gray thought as he made his way back to the portion of the Haystack Farm & Resort he'd rented, was what had him up at the crack of dawn. A hot woman camouflaged in a baggy running suit and surrounded by a circus of kids. He'd thought about her all night long. To the point where what sounded to him like someone strangling a rooster woke him just before he'd embarrassed himself with only the second wet dream of his life.

His feet crunched over the graveled walkway that led to the stables and Gray slowed down to a brisk walk. Stretching his arms above his head as he continued to move, he inhaled deeply and exhaled quickly, hoping the immediate slaps of cool air would erase the memories. All of them.

It didn't work. As he approached the steps Gray stopped. He did a series of three quick squats, then lowered his back leg and began stretching. She wasn't tall, he thought as he switched legs, his hands resting on his thigh as he lunged. Five feet and two or three inches tall, tops. She wasn't built, either. Her clothes had been loose but Gray had always been able to spot a great female body. Hers was tight, compact, curvy in all the right places and trim in the others. She had intelligent eyes and a stubborn chin. Her hair was short, styled but not overdone. Her face was cute, not gorgeous, but stick-in-the-mind pretty.

Gray sighed and stood up straight. He put his hands on his hips and let his head fall back as he looked up to the sky. No clouds, no sun, just a blanket of slate. Only one day in this small town and he missed Miami already.

He ran up the steps and let himself into the loft suite that carried the faint smell of the air fresheners that were plugged into every electrical socket in the space, and the earthier scents of hay and horseflesh. There were no five-star hotels in Temptation. Only two bed-and-breakfasts and this fully functional farm, which also billed itself as a resort. There were no televisions, either. No internet connection and no phones. The signal on his cell was weak, but the electrical outlets worked well enough so at least they kept his phone and tablet charged.

The shower worked, he thought with a frown. Thank the heavens for that. Stripping as he made his way back to the bathroom, Gray reminded himself why he was here.

To inspect the buildings and put them on the market. That was all.

When he stepped beneath the spray of hot water, he whispered again, "That is all."

But the moment he closed his eyes and tipped his head beneath the water, he saw her face. Big hazel eyes, a pert nose and small, very kissable lips. He'd wanted to kiss her as they'd been standing in that dark hallway. When he'd stepped closer to her it had been his intention to lean in and touch his lips to hers. It wasn't going to be gentle, rather demanding, hungry and needy. Gray dropped his head at the thought. He didn't need anyone. He never had.

If it was for sex, which his body was telling him with no uncertainty that it was, then he could call any number of women the moment he arrived back in Miami. He did not need to acknowledge his arousal around some small-town woman with a chip on her shoulder. Except that when she'd brushed up against him, his erection had come quick and hard, both times. Just that brush of her soft body against his had made him want her. Gray cursed. It had been a very long time since he'd wanted anything, or anyone.

He picked up the bar of soap and used the cloth he'd grabbed before entering the shower. Building a thick lather, he placed the soap back into the vintage silver tray and began to wash the sweat from his body. Only each stroke of that warm and sudsy cloth over his skin had him aching more with need. After the first few seconds Gray wanted to drop that cloth and wrap his hands around his burgeoning length. He wanted to stroke and stroke until there was a blessed release. His eyes opened quickly with that thought as he gritted his teeth and fought like hell to keep his hands on any other part of his body aside from his throbbing arousal.

When she'd looked up at him he'd wanted to whisper her name.

Morgan.

Morgan Hill.

She was just a woman.

Just a woman that he wanted to sink so deep inside of that everything about this dismal small town and what it had done to his family would be washed from his mind, once and for all. Gray had no idea if that would work, or if he even wanted to bother. Morgan had children, which meant there was most likely a father to those children in the picture somewhere. That was another entanglement Gray did not have the time or the inclination to manage.

With jerking movements he continued to wash and then rinsed beneath the steamy water. Once his shower was complete he dressed and sat at the little desk that faced the window. The view was breathtaking, if one liked such a thing. Gray did not. A country setting, simple living—neither was for him. He reached into his leather bag and pulled out the files he'd brought with him. Without internet access in this room, he would have uninterrupted time to go over his most recent sales projections and R&D reports. There was no doubt that once he logged into his email there would be numerous issues for him to address. Even on a Sunday morning.

His mother used to love Sundays, Gray thought as he stared down at the papers, then up to the window. She loved walking in the sand and watching the tide roll in just outside the house they'd lived in on Pensacola Beach. That was the only time Olivia Taylor had looked peaceful, Gray recalled. The only time after his father had left them.

"Hello?" Gray answered his cell phone, which had begun to ring loudly, snatching him out of his thoughts.

"Hi. How's it going?"

It was his sister Gemma. She was the oldest of the girls and the one Gray had been closest to since the two of them had taken care of the others when their mother began to get sick.

"Slowly" was his tired reply. "Apparently, the chamber of commerce doesn't open on Sundays. Nothing in this sleepy little town does."

"Weekends as a means of relaxation should be a crime," Gemma replied with her ready humor. "This is the only day of the week that I have all to myself so I don't want to hear one negative thing about it."

Gemma was a hair stylist. She owned one of the largest and most reputable salons in Washington, DC.

"I'm not complaining," Gray told her. "But I won't lie, if I could get this taken care of sooner, rather than later, I'd be much happier."

"I don't know that I've ever seen you happy, Gray," his sister said softly.

Oh, no, Gray thought with a shake of his head. They were not about to have this conversation. Gemma was the only one of his siblings who believed in the fairy tale of love, even though she'd yet to find her knight in shining armor. The fact that their mother had nursed a broken heart until her dying day didn't seem to matter to his sister. Gemma staunchly believed that love would always find a way. Gray usually allowed his sister her dream, but today he wasn't in the mood to humor her.

"First thing tomorrow morning I plan to march into city hall and speak with the rep at the chamber of commerce. It'll be good to get an idea of what the buildings are currently being used for."

"Why? I thought we were just going to sell them," Gemma replied. "You don't need that type of information to put them on the market."

Gray had thought of that last night as he'd left the community center. He hadn't needed to personally come back to Temptation, nor did he need an escort to show him around the buildings, either. It would have been much simpler to call his attorney and let him deal with the Realtors and the sale, an action he could have easily taken from his desk in his Miami office. There was just one thing stopping Gray from handling this the way he would any other business deal.

His mother.

"She would have wanted to know," he admitted quietly.

Gemma remained silent for a few seconds.

"She would have," she eventually agreed. "She'd always wanted to know about the town and how it was doing after we'd left. One of her greatest heartbreaks was that the loss of the money from our show and how the scandal that had followed our departure would have a negative effect on the town. She would have been happy to know the buildings were being used for something good, and she might not want us to sell them if they are."

Gray rubbed a hand over his forehead. "I've thought about all that, too. Garrek and Gen were on the fence about selling when I spoke to them," he said.

"Gia's trying to open another restaurant, so she says the money from the sale would come in handy," Gemma added.

"And Gage," Gray said before sighing as he thought about the youngest brother.

Gemma made a sound that mimicked his frustration with their brother. "He's so busy putting in hours at the hospital that he barely had time to sign that paper you had me take to him," she said and then sighed again. "It would have been a lot better if all of us could have gotten together and talked this through. Mama would not be happy knowing that it's been years since we were all in the same place, at the same time."

"We were born in the same place, at the same time," Gray stated drily.

"Now you sound like Gen, hating the way we came into this world."

Gray shook his head at that remark. "No, I don't hate that we were born. I just don't like all the attention that came afterward and the way this town that supposedly loved the Taylors of Temptation weren't there for us when everything came crashing down."

It didn't matter, Gray told himself immediately. When his mother decided to leave Temptation, her grandfather offered his vacation home in Pensacola Beach for her and the children to live in. His father, in a rare moment of generosity, hadn't contested the divorce or the spousal support and alimony payments. Eventually, years later, their family began to feel the benefit of Theodor's successful business endeavors through higher monthly payments. It was apparently much easier to write a check to his wife and six children than it was to live in the same house with them. The bottom line was that they hadn't needed anyone from this town back then and Gray definitely didn't owe them anything now.

"Look, I plan to have this wrapped up in the next day or so. I'll send a group email when the listings are up and then keep everyone posted on the sales."

"Right," Gemma said. "Business as usual. That's fine, Gray. I'll be sending out my gifts in the next couple of weeks, so be sure to check the mail at your condo."

Gray resisted the urge to sigh again. Instead, he squeezed the bridge of his nose. "You send us all Christmas gifts every year like you're our secret Santa. We're not kids anymore, Gemma."

"No," she said adamantly. "We're not. But Mama loved Christmas. She always had gifts for us under that tree no matter the circumstances. It's the least I can do to keep her alive in my heart, Gray. I know all of you have your way of dealing with the hand we were dealt in life, but this is mine so don't try to take it away from me."

After a few seconds of silence Gray replied, "I wouldn't think of it."

Gemma was right—she needed to deal with her life, in her way, just as the rest of his siblings did. Just as he did.

Gray ended the call with his sister and he was able to get lots of work done as the hours passed. Now, at close to six in the evening, he realized he hadn't eaten all day. Grabbing his jacket, Gray left the room and headed into town. He had driven to Virginia from Miami, deciding that he might enjoy the peace and quiet of the fifteen-hour drive. It was a drastic change from using his private jet to travel the globe and hiring drivers for the shorter distances when he traveled for business. This time it was personal, and Gray was certain he could handle maneuvering the streets of the small town.

That thought was short-lived. Almost an hour later, after going up and down street after street looking for a restaurant of his liking, Gray finally parked his car in front of Pearl's Diner on the corner of Sunset Drive and Evergreen Way. The first thing he noticed when he stepped out of his Porsche Panamera Turbo—besides the fact that the *i* and the *e* in *diner* were out on the lighted sign hanging in front of the establishment—was all the Christmas decorations. Thanksgiving had only been two days ago, but the holiday season was clearly in full swing in Temptation. Black lampposts positioned about six to eight feet apart had wreaths around the lighted tops and huge red ribbons in the center. Strung above the wires holding the street lights were large snowflakes formed from stencils and cheerful white lights. Funny, when he'd driven into town yesterday he hadn't seen any of this, or perhaps he hadn't wanted to see it. Could Gemma's earlier reference to how much his mother had loved Christmas be the cause of his revelation now?

Another reason he may not have noticed the decorations before—the more logical one that Gray preferred to consider—was that he'd avoided driving through the main streets of town when he arrived. Instead, he'd made a wrong turn the moment he entered the town from the highway, forcing his GPS to reconfigure the directions to the community center. That had worked just as Gray planned and he'd ended up traveling through narrow streets lined with houses before pulling up on Century Road, where the old planked structure of the community center sat on a corner. Gray hadn't wanted anyone to see him driving his fancy car through the old town. He recalled from his mother's stories how quickly news—good or bad—traveled in Temptation and how much the townsfolk enjoyed spreading such news.

Gray was still standing in front of the diner, looking at the holiday decorations, when he was approached by the first person in Temptation to lend credence to his mother's words.

"Well, aren't you a sight for these sore old eyes," a woman said. "You and that spicy little car you're driving."

She'd walked right up to him and now had a hand resting on his arm. Her perfectly coiffed dark brown hair was streaked with what looked like bronze in the front. Wrapped around her shoulders was some sort of black cape and she wore a festive red scarf.

"Good evening," Gray finally said, remembering once again how everyone in small towns thought they knew everybody else.

They'd all thought they knew how good a father and husband Theodor Taylor was, until the day he'd up and left his family in that big old house on Peach Tree Lane. So had Gray's mother, Olivia, and his siblings. That had been the moment of truth for Gray, one he would never forget, no matter how many years had passed, or how far away he managed to get from this town.

"You look awfully familiar," she said, squinting her eyes and moving in closer.

Her perfume was strong and her fingers clenched his arm a little tighter as if she thought the contact might jog her memory. For as much as Gray would like to have gone unnoticed a little while longer, he knew his presence would be made known eventually. Especially after he'd already introduced himself to the pretty woman at the community center last night.

"I'm Grayson Taylor and I'm just heading into the diner to have dinner," he told her.

"My word, Grayson Taylor," she said, a smile spreading instantly across her face. "The last time I saw you I don't think you came past here."

Here was the level near her thigh that she'd shown with a motion of her hand.

"How old were you then? Six or seven? That's when Olivia packed up and shuffled you poor children out of your home in the dark of night." She was shaking her head as she talked. "Shame the way she did that. You should have been allowed to grow up in your home, around the people that loved and cared about you all."

What she really meant was the people that loved all the revenue that the reality show his family had starred in brought to the town. The birth of the sextuplets had come at a time when Temptation was struggling to use its historic background to bring tourists and, subsequently, money into the town. The show had been a savior for the town, but a death sentence to his parents' marriage.

"I was seven years old back then, ma'am, and I really am hungry, so if you'll please excuse me," he said and attempted to walk away.

"Oh, don't go in there. Pearl doesn't work on Sundays.

Her daughter, Gail, does, but she's not as good a cook as her mama. You come on over to the hospital with me. They're having their annual charity ball and that food will be catered. Hopefully, it'll be better than Gail's since I know they paid this fancy new chef a ton of money."

She looped her arm around his and had started walking them across the street before Gray could accept or decline her offer.

"Ma'am, I'd rather not intrude," he began after a couple of steps.

"You can drop the *ma'am* and call me Millie. Millie Randall, that's what everybody around here calls me. And you're not intruding. We heard your daddy died a couple months back, poor fella. And with a young lady in his bed. At least that's what we heard." Millie whispered those last sentences.

She shook her head and continued before Gray could interject.

"So I suspect you're here about his properties. The hospital is one of them, so you might as well come on inside and see what you own."

First, Gray wasn't certain why the whispering was necessary, since they were the only two people outside at the moment. Second, her assumptions about his father's death were wrong and totally inappropriate, but still, he tried to keep his irritation under control.

"It's a pleasure to meet you, Mrs. Randall," he said because he'd already noted the gigantic diamond on her ring finger and he recalled Morgan mentioning her name last night. "I really don't think this is a good idea. I have other business to take care of."

"Always in a rush," Millie said with a shake of her head. She took two steps away from Gray and then turned back. "You get that from your mother. Olivia was always trying to move faster than she should have. Running to those fancy doctors and using all that money to produce that ungodly pregnancy."

"Wait a minute," Gray said, finally fed up with this woman and her comments.

He didn't give a damn who she was or where she worked. As he'd told Gemma earlier, he didn't need anyone in this town to show him the buildings he owned. He was simply trying to honor his mother's memory by coming back here and doing business as civilly as he could. That didn't mean he had to deal with any of this petty, small-town BS in the process.

"I'm here to handle current business, not to rehash the past," he told her curtly.

It was the best he could do, especially since instinct and habit were telling him to defend his mother and put this busybody in her place.

"Well, that's fine," she snapped and continued walking toward the building. "But we don't rush around in Temptation. It's not our way, so you'll just have to get used to that."

Gray frowned as he reluctantly walked behind her. He didn't want to get used to anything in Temptation.

Chapter 3

"You're just not used to being close to men anymore," Wendy said as she zipped the back of Morgan's dress.

Morgan turned away from the full-length mirror and closed the closet door it hung on. "I don't have a problem being around men, I just don't like arrogant and snobbish men," she replied.

After stewing about the issue all night she'd finally broken down and told Wendy about meeting Grayson Taylor last night. Lily and Jack were staying with her grandmother tonight, while she attended the annual holiday charity banquet at the hospital with Wendy. The event was to benefit the Widows and Orphans Fund, which had been started years ago by an anonymous mother who at one point had lost everything, but then came into a huge sum of money and wanted to give back. No one in town had ever seen this woman in person, but they'd accepted the money and agreed to continue the efforts, using each year's proceeds to help support single mothers with young children.

Wendy had worked at the hospital for the past five years. So Morgan had been attending this event before becoming a widow herself. She'd always believed in its purpose, and now, being a single parent, she knew firsthand how important it was to have assistance. In her corner were Granny and Wendy. Her parents had been gone since Morgan was a sophomore in high school, when her father received a job offer in Australia.

"I hear he's sexy as hell," Wendy continued.

She was standing near Morgan's dresser now, fluffing her loose curls. Her older sister was gorgeous, from her five-seven height to the generous curves she'd been blessed with and the bubbly personality that had landed her as captain of the cheerleading squad in high school. They shared the same creamy brown complexion and wide, expressive eyes, but that's where the similarities ended. Where Morgan loved the fall and Christmas carols, Wendy wanted to swim in the lake every day of the summer and detested the cold.

"All of them," she continued. "There are three boys and three girls. I don't think any of them signed over the rights for the show to go into syndication or onto DVD, but Granny told me just the other day how good-looking they all had grown up to be."

"And how would she know?" Morgan asked after she'd slipped her feet into the four-inch-heel platform red shoes that she'd treated herself to. "You know she hates the internet. That computer we bought her two years ago would have inches of dust on it if she wasn't such a neat freak."

Wendy shook her head. "And you know that's the truth," her sister agreed while laughing. "But you know her and Ms. Dessa love reading the tabloids down at the supermarket. She said there was a story about them a few months back when the father died."

Morgan pulled at the hem of the dress that she'd already

deemed too short. Wendy thought it was perfect—red, festive and flirty, she'd said. Morgan figured she was either going to freeze her buns off tonight trying to be cute, or fall flat on her face the moment she walked into the Olivia Taylor Hall at the hospital.

Olivia Taylor had been the equivalent of the Virgin Mary in Temptation. Thirty years ago, when she and her husband had been bold enough to travel to Maryland so that she could be artificially inseminated with multiple eggs, she'd shown every women in Temptation that it was okay to take their fate in their own hands. Morgan, and just about everyone who lived in Temptation, knew the story.

"They both need to find something else better to do during the day," Morgan said, grabbing her shawl from the bed and heading for the door.

Wendy laughed as she followed her out. "They need a man! Two of them, or maybe one and they can share."

Morgan shook her head. "You're ridiculous," she said.

The shawl would be for when she was inside the hospital. As for right now, her long wool coat was warranted as the temperature was expected to drop below freezing later that evening. While Morgan loved the season and the crisp cold winter air, she did not like shivering and shaking from the deep freeze that Temptation was known to receive this time of year.

"Not ridiculous, just practical," Wendy said while slipping into her short leather jacket. "What woman wouldn't want a nice handsome hunk of man to keep her warm on a night like this?"

Morgan stepped out into the evening air, recalling immediately how warm she'd felt each time Grayson had touched her. She continued walking to the car, feeling the cold breeze as it whipped through the air.

"I don't have any problem keeping myself warm," she

told her sister as she climbed into the passenger side of Wendy's SUV.

Still, she was shivering when she finally pulled the door closed, her traitorous body begging to differ.

"This wing of the hospital was named after your mother," Millie told Gray.

Her voice had begun to grate on him, like nails sliding over a chalkboard. She'd been talking, mixing historical facts about the town with quick jabs of gossip and innuendo, like they were part of some insider tour. If they were, Gray didn't want to partake—not a second longer.

"I think I've seen enough," he told her. He was certain that the twenty minutes that she'd taken to walk him around the hospital had been nineteen minutes too long in her company.

Based on this tour alone, he knew exactly what he would do once he finally found a spot with internet access. Gray would tell his attorney to sell, sell, sell! This town was just as bland and behind the times as he'd recalled and he would be glad to leave first thing tomorrow morning. Actually, he thought as Millie touched her jeweled fingers to his arm for about the billionth time, he would be more than glad.

"So you see, it makes sense for you to be here tonight at the charity event," she told him, blinking those unnaturally long lashes at him.

She'd been doing that as if she thought the action was somehow coercing him. It wasn't. Instead, that action and Millie's comments were beginning to irritate the hell out of him.

"I'm really not up for attending any type of event," he began. "Besides, I'm not dressed for anything formal."

"Oh, we rarely do formal here in Temptation. You should remember that," she chided, slipping her hand right through his arm again and turning him toward glass double doors at the end of the hallway.

The tiled floor was old here, just as Gray had noticed throughout the rest of the facility. There were a number of areas that could be refreshed and updated, he'd thought as he walked through. Windows could have better coverings, computers at the main desk on all of the floors looked to be at least ten years old, which in any field these days was not good. A hospital especially should have the most up-to-date equipment possible.

"You see we kept your mother's name right over the doors, just the way they were when we put them there years ago. She never did come back to see it, though. Her cousin, BJ, never understood that. She always thought Olivia was ungrateful, but you know how family can be," Millie continued as she walked him closer to those doors.

"It was very nice of the town to dedicate this portion of the hospital to my mother. I'm sure she was very grateful," Gray told her.

"Not enough to come back, though," Millie continued with a shake of her head. "But tonight's about new beginnings. We all start afresh with the New Year, so this charity dinner gives us a head start. You know, moneywise."

Gray nodded because that was another point Millie had made sure to hit home. The town needed money.

"Really," Gray said, coming almost to a stop before they could get closer to the doors. "I should get going. I have emails to send and calls to make."

Millie shook her head. "Always got something better to do. Just like your father. It's just a dinner, Grayson. And you said you were hungry, so come in, sit down and have a bite to eat. Then you can rush on and do what you have to do. But I'll tell you, if you're thinking of selling these buildings and running out on this town again, I beg you to think again. Whether you like it or not this is your heritage. It's where you were born and where your children should have a chance to grow up and experience all the things you never did."

"I don't plan on having children," Gray replied immediately.

He had no idea why he'd told her that, just felt the words slipping out without his permission.

Millie's smile spread slowly. "You never know what this world's got in store for you. Despite what your mother thought at first, she soon found out that everything doesn't always go as planned."

Gray was just about to tell her he was totally different from both his parents. He was going to assure her that she was wrong and that he would definitely not be getting married or having any children. Ever.

Then she approached. He'd heard the clicking of heels across the floor but hadn't bothered to look away from Millie until the other woman was standing right there behind the older one. He'd glimpsed at the bright red of her dress first, then realized how little material there actually was as his gaze soon rested on her stocking-clad legs. Then moved slowly to the swell of her pert breasts over the bodice. Her hair was tapered on the sides and curly on top, her makeup light, but alluring.

There was another woman with her, Gray noticed when he figured staring was probably just as rude as it was embarrassing on his part.

"Hi, Millie. You trying to keep all the handsome men out here with you tonight?" the third woman asked, her smile wide and her eyes cheerful as she looked at Gray.

She was a couple inches taller than Morgan, who he had noticed was wearing some pretty sexy heels tonight. The other woman also had on heels. Her hair was longer, curls relaxing on her shoulders as long, icicle-like earrings dangled and glowed. *Pretty* wasn't a bold enough word for this one and the tight black dress she wore, with a festive red choker that had small jingle bells dangling from it, was definitely something to stare at. Still, Gray's gaze went right back to Morgan.

"Not at all," Millie said, her smile faltering. "This is Grayson Taylor. You know, he's one of *the* Taylors of Temptation."

Gray didn't like that title any more than he liked the way Millie had said it—as if he was *the* Dracula of Transylvania.

"Hello, Grayson Taylor," the woman said as she extended her hand to him. "I'm Wendy Langston. I'm one of the Langstons of Temptation. We've been here forever, too, but most of us have done the smart thing and escaped as well." She chuckled and so did Gray, liking her instantly.

"Please," he said, taking her hand and shaking it. "Call me Gray."

"Well, Gray, you should come on in and join the fun. You can sit with me and my sister, Morgan. I hear Magnolia Daniels was this year's caterer. She just graduated from some fancy culinary college in New York, so she was anxious to come back home and show us all her skills," Wendy told him.

"My sister attended a culinary school in New York as well," he said. "She owns her own restaurant now and teaches at the college. I wonder if it's the same school Magnolia attended."

"There's only one way for us to find out," Wendy said as she easily stepped in front of Millie to snag Gray's arm.

This time, Gray wasn't as irritated. In fact, he thought, he could appreciate Wendy's cheerful demeanor. He could also like the fact that Morgan had looked a bit chagrined at the way her sister so easily stepped up to him.

They walked through the double doors that Gray had sworn he hadn't wanted to enter and he was pleasantly surprised, at least for a few moments. The lights were dim and there were tables all around the floor, covered in festive red cloths with what looked like little gingerbread houses in the center. Holiday music played softly in the background as fifty or so people walked around or hovered over the punch table.

"I'm going to get something to drink," he heard Morgan say and then looked up in enough time to see her walking hastily away from the table where Wendy had led him.

"I believe you've met my younger sister already," Wendy said as she took a seat in one of the folding chairs.

Gray sat in a chair beside her after he'd forced himself to look away from Morgan's retreating body.

"Yes. We met last night at the community center," he replied.

Wendy nodded. "You interrupted Jacob Marley's grand entrance in Mountainview Elementary's first-grade-class presentation of *A Christmas Carol*."

"Is that what they were doing?" he asked, then recalled the little boy named Ethan saying something about "bah, hamburger" when he'd taken his place on the stage after Gray first arrived.

"Yes. It's one of Morgan's favorites, so she begged the town council to let her class present the play, as opposed to the older members of the theater club, who had wanted to perform *The Sound of Music*. I think we're better off with the kids and that has nothing to do with my sister being the director," Wendy continued, chuckling again.

"I hope it turns out well," Gray responded.

He'd been wondering how long it was going to take Morgan to return. Not that he didn't like talking to her sister. Well, actually, Gray wasn't really in the mood to talk any more tonight. He did, however, want to be near Morgan Hill once again. That thought hadn't occurred to him earlier when he'd been busily immersed in his work. Yet,

the moment he saw her, he was unable—or unwilling…
he couldn't figure out which one just yet—to think about
anything else.

"It's going to be fun. You should think about sticking
around town to see the finished product."

This sister liked to talk. Gray was certain he hadn't gotten this many words out of Morgan the night before and
they'd been together longer. He looked at Wendy now, and
asked, "When is the production taking place?"

"Christmas Eve," she told him. "You weren't planning
on selling the community center before then, were you?"

Gray didn't immediately respond. Christmas was weeks
away. There was no way he planned on staying in town
for that long, and while he was immediately going to put
the buildings on the market, he wasn't optimistic that they
would sell so quickly. Who would want to buy run-down
buildings in this small town? There was no market value
to the purchases, only sentimental value, which he'd figured out from his talk with Millie, and Morgan's immediate reaction to finding out who he was.

"I don't think they'll be sold before Christmas," he answered. "Maybe I'll go help Morgan with the drinks."

Wendy had seemed to look at him knowingly as she replied, "Sure. You go right ahead and do that."

Regardless of what she said or thought about Gray as he
walked away, he kept moving. Too many people wanted to
chitchat with him in this town and he didn't want any of
that. What he wanted… Gray wasn't quite certain. Sure,
he'd thought he knew, just last night when he'd driven
into town, and earlier, when he talked to Gemma, but at
this moment…

Morgan turned away from the punch table just as he
walked up behind her. Quick footwork had him moving
just before she could turn with her outstretched hands,
which held two glasses filled with red punch. The red

punch that Gray had no doubt would have splashed all over his white shirt had they collided in the way they'd seemed destined to do.

"Let me help you with that," Gray offered and reached for one of the glasses.

She opened her mouth as if she was about to speak, then clapped her lips closed and allowed him to take the glass from her hand.

"Why don't we enjoy this over there near the tree," he said.

"That one is for my sister," she said, nodding toward the glass in his hand.

He shook his head and did not hesitate to lie. "She said she'd get something later."

"Why do you want to go over there? We can go back to our table," she said before lifting her glass to her lips and taking a sip.

"I want to be alone with you," he said, again without any hesitation.

Or any thought to what he was doing. All Gray could admit to with any sort of definitiveness was that he wanted to be with Morgan. His salacious thoughts from last night were at the forefront of his mind as he stood close to her, the light scent of her perfume wafting through the air.

"And I like Christmas trees," he continued when she only glared at him, one brow lifted in silent question.

"Lily said you didn't like Christmas," she replied after another few moments of silence.

"Your daughter," he said when he remembered the solemn-faced little girl from last night. "She and your son are twins, correct?"

Morgan nodded. "They're the loves of my life," she replied, then looked up quickly as if she hadn't meant to say that.

Gray decided to let it slide because there was another

pressing question he wanted an answer to. "And their father? Is he also the love of your life?"

For the first time ever Gray held his breath as he waited for the answer.

Her fingers seemed to tighten around the glass she held before she replied, "My husband died in Afghanistan."

It was a simple statement and yet it held as much power as if she'd reached out and socked him herself.

"I'm sorry to hear that," he said.

Gray moved beside her then, taking her elbow lightly, and began to walk toward the tree. "Do you like Christmas?"

"What?" she asked as they moved.

"Do you like Christmas? That's what Lily asked me last night. Now I want to know your answer."

"Yes, I love Christmas," she said before taking another sip of her punch.

Gray hadn't bothered to sip his.

"It's a wonderful time of year. A time for family and fellowship, miracles and happiness."

"You sound like one of those greeting-card commercials," he replied.

"And you sound like the star of my play, Ebenezer Scrooge," she snapped back.

They'd come to a stop near the huge Christmas tree that was nestled in a far corner of the room. It had to be at least ten feet tall and was decorated with what looked like every sort of bulb, bell, ribbon and light ever created for this season.

"I don't have anything in particular against the holiday," Gray confided. He'd walked farther around the tree toward the side that was facing two large windows.

The old window shades were tattered at the edges and if anyone attempted to pull them down farther, they'd surely crumple into pieces. So more than half the window was bare, leaving a view of the side street, where only two cars were parked and the sidewalk was clear. At this time of evening on a Sunday night, if Gray had looked out the window of his penthouse in Miami he was sure to see lines of traffic and people headed toward the clubs or the beach. There was always something going on in the city, some party or meeting, a huge wedding, or a celebrity sighting. Never a dull moment, and never a quiet street like this.

"Do you normally spend the holiday with the rest of your family?"

Gray lifted his head to see Morgan standing right beside him. She'd put her glass down on the windowsill and he did the same before thinking about an answer to her question. He hadn't thought of his siblings in the traditional sense of the word *family*. The fact that they each lived in different states could be the reason for that. They'd been born together and had lived together for eighteen years. They were the closest thing to friends Gray had ever had, and the only ones who shared the same dark disappointments of the past with him.

"No. My sisters and brothers have their own lives," he replied.

"There are six of you—surely you find time to spend with each other at some point. I only have one sister and it seems like we're never apart," she told him.

She looked across the room and Gray followed her gaze. More people had come in, filling up the tables. The sound of numerous voices had grown a bit louder. The instrumental holiday music still sounded over the guests' voices and Gray found himself thankful for the partial privacy of this corner. He didn't want to talk to any of the people out there, but here, on this side of the tree with all its twinkling lights reflecting off the window, he was content to stand with this woman.

"Yes, there are six of us. I'm the oldest. Born almost

immediately after me were Garrek, Gemma, Genevieve, Gage and Gia. Once we turned eighteen we all went our separate ways."

"And you don't keep in touch? That's not good. I mean, it's kind of sad. I would think that you would be closer," she said, then clamped her lips shut again.

Gray shook his head. "It's not a problem. A lot of people think a lot of things about the Taylor sextuplets. They have since the first airing of that damn television show. None of them know the truth."

"You sound as if the truth is sad," she replied quietly.

Gray shrugged. "It is what it is."

She nodded. "Just like you selling the buildings, I guess."

Her back was to the window and Gray moved to stand in front of her. He rubbed the backs of his fingers lightly over her cheek.

"Those buildings mean something to you, don't they?" he asked her.

She shrugged this time, shifting from one foot to the other as if his proximity was making her nervous. Being this close to her was making him hot and aroused. He wondered if that's what she was really feeling as well.

"This town means something to me. There are good people here and we're trying to do good things."

"That's what my mother used to say," Gray continued, loving the feel of her smooth skin beneath his touch. "Temptation was a good place. Love, family, loyalty. They meant something to the town. Always. That's what she used to tell us when we were young. But that was after the show, after my father found something better outside of this precious town of Temptation."

Gray could hear the sting to his tone, felt the tensing of his muscles that came each time he thought about Theodor Taylor and all that he'd done to his family. Yes, Gray had buried his father two months ago. He'd followed the old man's wishes right down to the ornate gold handles on the slate-gray casket, but Gray still hated him. He still despised any man who could walk away from his family without ever looking back.

"Show me something better," he said as he stared down into Morgan's light brown eyes. "Show me what this town is really about and maybe I'll reconsider selling."

"Are you making a bargain with me?" she asked. "Because if you are, I don't know what to say. I'm not used to wheeling-and-dealing big businessmen like you."

"I'm asking you to give me a reason why I shouldn't sell those buildings. Just one will do. If you can convince me—"

She was already shaking her head. "I won't sleep with you, if that's what you mean by *convince* you."

Gray blinked. That wasn't what he'd meant and the vehement way in which she'd made that declaration had scraped his ego raw.

"I didn't ask you to sleep with me," he told her and took a step closer. "But if I did…" He purposely let his words trail off, the tip of his finger sliding closer to the edge of her lips.

"I'd still say no. I don't sleep with uptight businessmen," she told him, that stubborn chin of hers jutting forward.

If she could have, Gray was certain she would have backed all the way out of that window to get away from him. That wasn't going to happen, especially not when he snaked an arm around her waist and pulled her closer to him, until she was flush against his chest the same way she had been last night when she'd bumped into him. He liked her right there, liked the heat that immediately spread throughout his body with her in this position.

"Don't worry," he whispered. "I won't ask you. I don't

sleep with small-town women with chips on their shoulders."

"I'm not—" she began but Gray quieted her words by touching his lips immediately to hers.

White-hot heat seared through him at the touch. His tongue swooped inside, taking her by surprise. A warm and delicious surprise that had him wrapping his other arm around her and holding her tight. Her hands came around to his back, clenching the material of his suit jacket as she opened her mouth wider to his assault. They were consuming each other, right here in the corner of this room at the hospital where Gray and his siblings had been born.

He wanted to turn her just a little, to press her back against the wall and take her right here, just like this. He could feel how hot she was and could imagine that same heat pouring over him as she came. She would wrap her legs around him, her short but strong legs would hold him tightly, keeping him securely embedded inside her. They would be short of breath, but love every second of their joining. It would be the best sex…no, it would be really good sex, for Gray, something he hadn't indulged in often enough.

It would be… Something moved at his side. It made a noise and moved again. She stilled in his arms, then abruptly pulled back. Gray was cursing as he realized what was moving was his vibrating cell phone. With a frown Gray pulled it out of his pocket and looked down at the text on the lighted screen. He would have never considered that Morgan might look down as well.

"I'll let you go tend to Kym," she said icily, before stepping around him and making a hasty exit.

Chapter 4

The Sunnydale Bed-and-Breakfast was a stately white colonial with black shutters nestled in the center of a cul-de-sac and surrounded by a number of beautifully mature trees. Gray admitted the next afternoon as he approached the dwelling that it looked as if it should be featured on a postcard boasting the simplicity of small-town living. The American flag flying high above the black double doors and brick walkway slammed home the patriotic angle, while chubby shrubs lined the perimeter with the precise planning of a *Better Homes and Gardens* portrait. Once inside, the historic charm continued with scuffed wood-planked floors, emerald-green-and-white textured wallpaper stretching throughout the front foyer and along the wall next to a winding glossed cherry-wood railing.

There was just enough of the new world interspersed with the old, as the front desk clerk had spoken to Gray after hanging up the telephone and was taking an inordinately long time to type a reservation into a computer.

"I'm here to see Kym Hutchins. I believe she has a room here," Gray told the clerk, who was staring at him over gold wire-rimmed glasses.

"Well, I'll be damned," the older gentleman began. "Millie wasn't lying after all."

"Pardon me?" Gray asked even though he had a hunch what was about to take place.

The man shook his head before coming around the desk to stand right in front of Gray. He wore tan pants that were at least three sizes too big, held up by black suspenders, which again, didn't really fit him well, but were drawn so tight they looked almost painful on his shoulders. His short-sleeved dress shirt was a lighter shade of tan, and a wrinkled handkerchief poked out of his breast pocket. His skin was a very weathered almond color, while his hair—what was left of it—was short, gray and curled close to his scalp.

"You're one of the Taylors, all right. Tall and broad just like your daddy was," the man said as he continued to look Gray up and down. "Got some fancy clothes on, too. I know because no stores in Temptation even carry dress pants with studs at the bottom, or shirts with those fancy gold cuffs you're wearing. Nowhere to go in town where you gotta be that sharp, unless it's in your own casket."

Gray frowned. People in this town said whatever came to their mind, whenever they saw fit. It was a good thing Temptation was still somewhat thriving because its people wouldn't make it in the big city.

"Sir, if you'll be so kind as to let Ms. Hutchins know that I'm here," Gray said, again employing all his patience to deal with the older members of this town.

"Oh, she's already waiting in the parlor. Came down in her fancy dress and par-r-r-fume," he said, mispronouncing and dragging the word out until it sounded totally ridiculous.

Ridiculous and just a little bit funny, as the man's face

had contorted in a way that Gray presumed was his rendition of being upper class.

"Then I'll just go on in and see her," Gray said and turned to the right to go through a walkway.

"The parlor's this way," the man told Gray.

He'd turned and walked, his posture a little bent over, toward double pocket doors to the left.

"Guess you two got someplace to go all dressed up like you are," he continued. "I don't reckon any man around here wears suits and ties on a daily basis. And the women, they don't wear skirts with matching jackets unless they're going to church. Me, I don't go anywhere I need to put on shiny suit jacket and shave. Used to tell my Ethel that all the time. If I go to church I put on pants and a shirt. I brush my teeth and my hair and I'm done. She never understood, but she never left me, either."

He was chuckling so hard, Gray thought he might actually tip over from the effort. He stood close just in case that did happen. Instead, the man began to wheeze just as they stepped into the parlor, which had a plush burgundy carpet.

"Ma'am, you got a beau come to see you," he told Kym.

"Thank you, Otis," Kym said when she stood from the spot where she'd been sitting.

"You're quite welcome, ma'am," Otis replied and turned to leave.

Gray glanced at the man once more, trying to figure out if he was really blushing or if there was some other health condition going on.

"She's a looker," Otis whispered, his bushy eyebrows dancing up and down as he grinned.

Gray couldn't help but smile—the man might be old in years, but he hadn't lost a step when it came to women.

Kym Hutchins was indeed a good-looking woman. She was tall at five foot nine and a half inches, with a slim figure, a light golden complexion and long black hair that was always perfectly styled. Her makeup was flawless, as usual, her legs long in the knee-length navy blue skirt with the matching jacket, which perfectly accented her sophisticated and professional demeanor. She was a very intelligent woman and she was his executive assistant. None of which explained why she was here in Temptation.

"Hello, Grayson," Kym said when Otis had meandered away, leaving them alone in the cozy parlor.

There were heavy-looking drapes hanging almost from floor to ceiling in a strange mustard color and four round mahogany tables with matching chairs around them. In the center of each table was a bouquet of roses, in the exact shade that was on Kym's lips as she gave him a brilliant smile.

"Hello," he replied. "I'm not sure how you knew I was here. I didn't put anything on my calendar."

With a flick of her hand, the large curls that had been draped over her shoulders were pushed back as her chin tilted slightly.

"I came by your place to drop off the Miago contracts but you weren't there. When I spoke to your doorman he indicated that you'd taken the Porsche and said you would return in a week. I know you've been handling your father's estate so I took an educated guess," she told him.

"And you showed up without me inviting you? Without letting me know your intentions?" Gray wasn't certain how he should feel about that.

"Why don't we have a seat, Grayson. Otis is going to bring us a beverage. I asked for wine spritzers but he politely informed me that this establishment does not sell or serve alcoholic beverages. Can you imagine?" she asked with a shake of her head.

Kym was already taking a seat, crossing her long, bare legs as she did. Gray figured it made sense to sit and talk to her, even though he was still trying to figure out why she'd come all this way in the first place.

"Did you know they don't have any hotels in this town?" With that said, Kym let out a short sigh. "I don't know what they do with the tourists, whenever they get them."

"They have two B and Bs and a resort," he told her, keeping it to himself that the resort was actually a farm.

"No four-star hotels, no wine. It's a wonder they're still functioning at all," she replied.

Gray didn't speak, but let his hands rest on his thighs as he continued to stare at her. "Did you bring the contracts with you?"

"My briefcase is in my room. Since you sent a text indicating that we would meet later, rather than first thing this morning as I'd presumed, I thought we'd have a drink and catch up first." She talked as she pulled her tablet from a large designer bag that she had sitting in a chair next to her.

Gray had taken his time getting over there, part of the reason being he still wasn't certain why she'd come.

"There's a phone conference with Tokyo on Thursday. Are you still going to make that? Should I have them call you at…wait, where are you staying?"

Kym looked up at him just as Gray was staring at a painting hanging on the wall between the two large windows. It was of an African American couple, perhaps taken in the early 1900s as evidenced by the style of dress the woman was wearing and the bowler hat worn by the man, who was sitting down. Trees and grass covered the background of the piece. The couple looked anything but happy and Gray found himself wondering who they were and what their story was. Normally, such a thing would not have intrigued him—the emotional state of people not being high on his list of priorities. He'd learned long ago that a person could go for years and years hiding their true feelings. Still, this couple piqued his interest. Enough so that Kym had reached over the table and was now pulling on his jacket sleeve as she called his name.

"Yes?" he replied curtly to her and then had to take a deep breath and start over. "What were you saying?"

She blinked several times as if he'd spoken a foreign language and then Gray could actually see her pulling herself together. It was in the straightening of her shoulders, the slow setting of her hands on the sides of her tablet and the careful way in which she spoke.

"I asked where you're staying. They said there was only one room left here when I checked in last night, but when I asked if you were here they said no. Actually, the woman who had been on duty just about laughed at my question," Kym said.

"I have a room at the resort," he told her curtly. "I can sign the contracts today and you can head back to Miami. What time is your flight out?"

Temptation did not have an airport so she had to have driven here, or taken a taxi from Dulles International Airport. It would have been a town car, he thought, and she would have charged it to her expense account because that's how Kym rolled. No way was she driving—even though she owned a Mercedes S550, she never went farther than from her apartment to the office on any given day.

"I didn't book a return flight," she replied. "I figured we'd return together and since I didn't know your plans I waited. Are you finished wrapping up your father's estate? I told Philip to be on standby in case you needed him."

Philip Stansfield had been Grayson's personal and business attorney for more than ten years.

"No. I'm not finished and I'll contact Philip if I need him," he told her.

She reached across the table once more, touching Gray's arm again. His gaze fell to her hand this time as she spoke quietly.

"You do not have to go through this alone, Grayson. I've been with you for six years and I've never heard you mention your father. So I know this might not be the easiest task for you."

Gray was just about to respond. He was trying to figure out a cordial way to ask her to stop touching him. She'd never touched him this much in the past. Before he could speak another hand appeared. A smaller one, with light pink painted fingernails. She wrapped those little fingers around two of Gray's and said, "Hello."

He looked over to see Lily standing there, her hair pulled back into one ponytail today, with a green-and-white ribbon at the top. When she looked at Gray she smiled. He couldn't help it—he smiled, too.

"Hello, Lily," he said, moving his arm so that Kym's hand slipped away and his grip tightened on Lily's hand.

"Are you having tea?" she asked.

"No. I don't think so," Gray replied.

"This is the room where people have tea. That's what Nana Lou said."

"Nana Lou?"

Lily nodded. "Uh-huh, she's in the kitchen. I was helping her make dough, but my hands were tired."

"I see. Where is your mother?" Gray asked.

"At work," Lily replied and then turned to Kym and asked, "Who are you?"

Gray turned to his assistant to see her staring down at Lily as if she was some type of anomaly. Kym's pert nose had crinkled, her dislike apparent until she caught Gray looking at her.

"Ah, hello, little one," she said before clearing her throat. "My name is Ms. Hutchins and I'm with Mr. Taylor."

Now he was Mr. Taylor. Gray tried not to show his confusion. "She works with me, Lily. How about I take you back out to the kitchen with Nana Lou."

Lily shook her head. "I want to stay here and have tea with you and her."

"My name is Kym Hutchins and we're not having tea. We're talking. You know, adult talk, so you can run along now," Kym told Lily with a wave of her hand as if the little girl needed the direction.

Gray stood then, lifting Lily into his arms. Behind him he thought he heard Kym gasp, but he didn't turn around.

"Sure, we can have tea together. Let's see if Nana Lou will make it for us," he said as he began walking out of the parlor, only to be stopped when Lily greeted Morgan loudly.

Morgan didn't know what to say.

Gray was holding Lily in his arms.

They looked, well, for lack of a better word, happy.

"Hi, baby," she said after another second of silence. "What are you doing out here with Mr. Taylor?"

She lifted her arms and welcomed her daughter into her embrace. She smelled like cinnamon rolls and icing, Morgan thought as Lily held her tightly around the neck. Lily was always glad to see Morgan when they'd been apart, as if she thought there was a chance she might not see her again. The twins had barely been two when James died, but sometimes Morgan thought they remembered that exact day he'd left them, the same way that she did.

"I'm taking a break," Lily told Morgan. "We're gonna have some tea. Me, Ms. Kym and, Mr. Gray?"

"He's Mr. Taylor," Morgan said, correcting her daughter.

"She can call me Mr. Gray," he said with a smile.

He still stood very close to Morgan, one hand slipped into the pocket of the crisply pleated black pants of his suit.

His shirt was bright white, just as it had been last night, but today's tie was an icy-blue color. There was no question that this man looked phenomenal in a suit. Nor was there any question that the kiss they'd shared last night had kept Morgan up into the early-morning hours. She silently chastised herself. It was just a kiss. That was all.

Then why was Gray looking at her as if he knew exactly what she was thinking and that he begged to differ—that their kiss was... definitely *something*?

"Hello," a woman said.

Morgan shook her head and looked away from Gray. Coming to stand beside him was a gorgeous woman with a frosty smile and assessing eyes. Morgan instinctively tightened her grip on Lily as she cordially said, "Hello."

"You have a lovely daughter," the woman volunteered. "Grayson and I work together. We were taking care of some business when this little one showed up."

Morgan had to blink to keep the words running through her mind from spilling out. Was this woman serious? Did she have an attitude about Lily being there?

"Lily and I were going to get some tea," Gray added, without looking at the woman at his side.

Wait, did Lily say Ms. Kym? Morgan held back her frown, along with the smart remark she'd already been trying to keep to herself. So this was the Kym who had sent Gray that text message last night. The one who had said simply, "I'm here in town. Call me."

"That's fine, you get back to your business. I'll take Lily out of your way," Morgan told Gray.

She hadn't bothered to look at Kym again, either, until the woman spoke one more time.

"That would be wonderful. Please let the staff know that we'd like some privacy. Thank you."

As if it was that simple to command someone to do her bidding, Kym turned away and pulled out a chair to have a seat at one of the tables. Morgan stared at Gray, who she thought looked like he wanted to say something to this Kym person. If that was the case, he was taking too long.

"Oh, you must be mistaken," Morgan said to her. "I don't work here, nor do I work for Mr. Taylor. My daughter and I will be going now."

She was out of the parlor and had just dropped a kiss on Lily's forehead when Gray touched her arm.

"You keep running from me," he said in an irritated tone.

Not wanting to make Lily think that something was wrong, Morgan slowly eased away from Gray, until his hand was dropping away from her arm.

"Not running, leaving. You're busy with work and I have to get Jack," she told him.

"You ran out on me last night," he said, his brow furrowing as if he was still trying to figure out why.

Well, he didn't have to try any longer—Morgan planned to tell him, but then Lily moved and she remembered that her daughter would hear everything she said, so she bit her tongue once more.

"We were finished last night. You're the one who chose not to stay for dinner," she replied. "Or rather, you're the one who had someplace else to be."

Gray's lips thinned into a straight line as he, too, looked down at Lily.

"What about what we were discussing last night?" he asked her finally.

Morgan had thought about that during the night as well. He'd said if she could give him a reason that he shouldn't sell the buildings, he wouldn't. Which was the exact reason why she'd been grateful when Harry asked to pick up the children after school today. She'd gone to the chamber of commerce to meet with Millie. Armed with all she needed to know about the buildings that Gray owned and a bit more, she felt like she was more than ready to show him why he should leave Temptation and those buildings alone forever.

"Whenever you're ready for me to present my case, let me know," she said.

"I'm ready right now," Gray responded.

Morgan shook her head, then looked to the doorway of the parlor to see Kym standing there.

"I have to get to the community center for rehearsal and then home to bed because we have school tomorrow. On Tuesdays and Wednesdays the theater club has the center for their rehearsals, so we won't rehearse tomorrow. I can meet you at your parents' house at six."

He frowned and Morgan realized it was probably because she'd called the old Victorian "his parents' house." After what Millie had told her—the parts that Morgan had deemed true, despite all the rest that Millie had thrown in—she could sort of understand why Gray didn't hold much love for that house, or this town for that matter. Still, she had enough love for Temptation to try and save what they were already starting to build.

"Is that time all right with you, or will you still be working?" she asked and refused to look at Kym, who she knew was listening to every word they said.

Gray took a deep breath then let it out slowly, so that his broad shoulders moved slightly. A part of Morgan wanted to hear his side of the story. She wanted to know why his father had really left his family and why Gray's mother thought her only recourse was to leave the town that had been her home. More importantly, Morgan found herself wondering about Gray and the man he had become. Feeling a quick spurt of guilt, she looked away from him.

"It's fine," he said immediately, as if he thought she might be ready to renege on her offer.

She nodded and turned away, alarmed at the fact that

she had been about to tell him to forget it. How could she continue to be in this man's company when every time they were together he switched on something inside her that she'd thought she'd buried years ago with her husband? Every. Damn. Time.

Chapter 5

"Hi, Morgan. Why didn't you call me? I would have brought the children over to the community center," Harry said the second Morgan entered the front foyer.

She hadn't seen him standing there on the other side of the steps and was just about to walk past him when he spoke.

"Oh, hi, Harry. That's okay. You've done enough. I really appreciate you picking them up and watching them for me," Morgan said.

Morgan had known Harry since they were little kids. He'd grown into a tall man, broadly built with a dark-chocolate complexion, bald head and warm smile. He was the oldest of three children born to Louisa and Clyde Reed and one of the most reliable people that Morgan knew. He also had a crush on Morgan, at least that's what Wendy had said for years. Morgan had always considered Harry a friend. That's all. Besides, she hadn't thought about another man romantically since James's passing. Until Gray. She shook her head again to clear the wayward thoughts that had been plaguing her these last couple of days.

"You know it's no problem," Harry said. "Where'd you run off to, little lady?" he asked Lily.

She still clung tightly to Morgan.

"I heard voices and then I saw Mr. Gray. I wanted to have tea with him," Lily announced as if that was as normal as saying she wanted to watch *Doc McStuffins* on television.

Morgan wished she hadn't said it and Harry looked confused.

"She's talking about Grayson Taylor," Morgan told him. "He's in the parlor with his, um…a woman he works with. He's been in town for a couple of days. Lily met him when he stopped by the community center a couple of nights ago."

Harry had only nodded while she spoke, his brow creasing. "So the rumors are true. He's gonna sell those buildings and add to the millions he's already got."

"He may not sell them," Morgan said, then wished she hadn't.

Harry frowned down at her. "How do you know what he's going to do?"

She shrugged. "I'm going to try to talk him out of it."

"What? You don't know him. You don't know men like him at all, Morgan. You should just steer clear and let him do what he needs to do and be gone."

"I can't do that," Morgan said.

Jack came running into the room at that moment and Morgan hastily grabbed his hand.

"Thanks again, Harry," she said. "I've got to get going."

Morgan walked through the front doors and down the walkway to her car. She didn't look back, as she was sure to find Harry staring at her.

* * *

The next afternoon, when Gray climbed out of his car to flashing lights and questions being hurled at him from at least three reporters, he wanted to reach out and punch somebody in the face. Of course, he resisted that urge, especially since two of the reporters were women.

They'd been following him around town since he'd walked out of the coffee shop where he'd met Kym for coffee and bagels that morning.

"I can talk to them if you want," Kym had offered when they'd walked to his car.

"I don't have anything to say to them and that means you don't, either," he told her.

"But they're here to see what you plan to do for your hometown this time. Your family was so instrumental in helping to revitalize the town thirty years ago, the people here are hoping you'll do the same. The press is eating all this up, which you know is going to be great for the launch in a couple of months."

Gray Technologies was launching a new cell-phone-and-tablet combo that was small and slim enough to fit into a wallet. Its battery life and network range was triple that of the strongest and most popular product on the market. It was one of the biggest and brightest inventions yet, so yes, Gray had to admit it was a huge deal. But not big enough to sell his soul to the devil that was the press. He'd hated them all his life and avoided them like the plague, relying solely on his PR department to deal with all media coverage. He didn't plan to stop now.

"I don't know how they knew I was here," he said.

"Does it matter? They're here and so are you. This is free advertising, Grayson. No matter what you decide to do here, it's a win-win for us," Kym had insisted.

Gray had only shaken his head and climbed into his car

just as one of the reporters had skirted around Kym and pressed a microphone in his face.

"Tell us how it feels to be back in your hometown, Grayson?" the reporter had asked just before Gray slammed his car door shut.

He spent the rest of the day closed in his room at the resort, reading more of his reports and thinking steadily about his meeting with Morgan later that day.

It would be the first time he walked into the house where it had all begun. There'd been happiness and excitement as his parents had waited for the birth of the sextuplets. The town had shared in the anxiety of watching Olivia waddle to church, to the grocery store, to visit with her family and then back to the big house to wait a little more. When the babies finally came, so had the press. Then came the cable television station that had offered the Taylors more money than they'd ever dreamed of to let cameras follow them around day in and day out.

The money was for the medical bills and to put into college funds for each of the children. That's what his mother had told him one day when Gray was a teenager. It was a wonderful plan to ensure their children had the very best of everything, she'd said as her gaze had lingered on the rolling waves. She loved the water at the beach, but Gray knew that his mother had loved this little town much more.

The hours had passed quickly enough and Gray, without the help of his PR people, had called the front desk of the resort to ask about a back way out of their property. Netta Coolridge, the owner's sixteen-year-old daughter, had come to his room carrying a tray of covered dishes, which gave the impression of him having a large meal. Instead, she'd smiled as she lifted one of the domed covers to reveal a thick length of rope.

"What's that?" Gray asked as he looked from the rope back to Netta's smiling face.

"It's how I get out of the house without my parents knowing," she replied with a brilliant, braced-teeth smile.

She was a cute girl with high cheekbones and long, straight honey-gold hair on one side. The other side was shaved like a man's, with a row of four curving lines that showed her scalp. She wore jeans and a hooded sweatshirt with the logo of a popular teen clothing store etched across the front.

"This window will lead you down to the back of the stalls. Your car is parked right on the side. It's already getting dark so if you stay close to the wall in the shadows those nosy reporters won't see you."

Netta talked as she walked across the room to open one of the windows. She'd taken the rope with her and tied a knot as she wrapped it around the leg of the massive armoire lodged in the corner.

"Mama insists on feeding those rude vultures and she's just about finished with the spaghetti and meatballs she prepared. She offered to let them come inside and eat, but they already told her they needed to keep watch. So I'll go back down and start bringing the fixings out to them, while you sneak out."

"Wait a minute," Gray asked, confusion giving way to incredulity at this point. "You expect me to climb down a window and sneak to my car? I've never done such a thing in my life," he told her.

When she'd dropped the other end of the rope out the window, Netta turned to him and shrugged. "Well, there's a first time for everything," she quipped.

Gray had discarded his suit jacket and slipped a sweater over his dress shirt this time. He grabbed his leather bomber jacket and was pushing his arms into it as he shook his head. "I'm not ducking and hiding from these people," he declared.

Netta shook her head and made a tsking sound with her

teeth. "Suit yourself," she told him. "But I counted five news vans and two cars when I came over. They're not in the driveway because Daddy threatened to shoot any of them that parked on our land, but they're right down there by the front gate. If you want to, you can drive right on out that way and see how far you get. Me, I'd get to shimmying out that window and take the back road along the creek to avoid them."

She was walking past Gray now, and stopped to clap a hand on his shoulder. "But you handle it your way, city slicker, and let me know how that works out for you."

The knowing grin that spread across her face as she turned for the door both amused and annoyed Gray. He was frowning by the time he grabbed his phone and keys and headed toward the window.

Now, forty minutes later, he was getting out of his car when the reporters flanked him once more. A threat to sue their newspaper and a reminder that he was about to be on private property had them quickly backing up.

Gray was about to walk up the broken bricked pathway to the house where he'd spent the first seven years of his life. There was a tear at the bottom of his left pant leg from jumping down after climbing out the window and down the rope. He'd gotten caught on one of the bushes that Netta neglected to tell him were circling the building. She had been right about him making a quiet getaway using that back road—as far as Gray could tell, none of the reporters had followed him back into town.

It was chilly tonight and this part of Peach Tree Lane was untouched by the Christmas decorations and holiday cheer. Gray didn't know how he felt about that, just as he wasn't sure how this meeting was going to go. The place looked the same, he thought as he came closer to the front steps. He couldn't see all the details of the house. It sat in the shadows of early evening almost like one of those haunted houses used for horror movies. With his hands thrust into the pockets of his jacket, he gazed up, not yet ready to take the stairs and walk along the wood-planked porch.

Yes, it was the same, he thought. The feeling that he'd always had when he was there. Warmth spread throughout his chest without his permission. Sounds of little boys rolling toy trucks up and down that porch while little girls took turns on the tire swing that used to hang from that huge oak tree to his left echoed in his mind. Food would be cooking by now because it was close to dinnertime. On the grill in the backyard, because that's where Dad liked to stand and show the cameras how he prepared a BBQ supper for his family. That was only one of the falsehoods that Theodor Taylor perpetuated.

"Sorry to keep you waiting," Morgan said as she came up to stand beside him. "I've got a key if you don't have one. Millie gave it to me yesterday when I met with her."

It took a moment for Gray to remind himself of the present. His quick look into the past left a bitter taste in his mouth.

"Does the head of your chamber of commerce always give citizens keys to properties that don't belong to them?" he asked and bristled at the chill in his tone.

Morgan pursed her lips and replied, "Millie's husband, Fred, owns the property management company that's been keeping this place from falling down over the years. When I told her I planned to show you around town, she was the one who suggested I start here. Fred agreed and offered me the key."

Disappointed in the fact that he seemed to be taking his bad mood out on her, Gray only nodded at first. He looked up to the house again—even in the growing darkness he could see the loose shingles on the roof.

"I don't have a key, so I suppose their foresight works out," he said.

"I suppose it does" was Morgan's response as she moved past him and started up the steps.

She wore jeans tonight, dark ones that fit quite nicely over the curve of her backside, and a white puffy coat that made her look like a snowball at the top. Gray followed behind her and only hesitated slightly before walking through one of the two red doors. He'd never liked that stark and bold color against the pale blue of the house, but ignored it now as he stepped inside, the old wood floors squeaking beneath his weight.

"They keep the power on," Morgan said as she switched on the lights. "Fred said they'd been in contact with someone from your father's legal team last year. They were talking about converting the house into a museum."

Gray was busy looking around. On either side there were archways leading into separate rooms. The room to the right served as their playroom, while the space on the left was the formal living room. Large area rugs had covered the majority of the wood floors—which at that time still gleamed from his mother's care.

"What? A museum? Are you serious?" he asked as her words finally registered.

She unzipped her coat while skirting around him to close the door that he'd left open behind them.

"Yes," she said. "Apparently, your father wanted to commemorate all that he and your mother had gone through to get pregnant. There was supposed to be a new wing at the hospital dedicated to the study of obstetrics, employing doctors who specialized in fertility options and multiple births."

"My brother Gage specializes in that area," Gray said, still frowning as he tried to understand exactly what she was telling him.

Morgan began walking ahead of him. She moved farther through the foyer, passing the stairs that were still lined in the forest green carpet. As children they'd always wanted to slide down the railings, but since the steps turned sharply to the left, it had been out of the question.

"In addition to the new wing at the hospital, your father's plan was to have this house show all the milestones you and your siblings made while you were here. Apparently, there'd been a deal in the works with another television network, to do a sort of where-are-they-now segment."

"Why didn't I know about this?" Gray asked as they made their way toward the back of the house. "How can they do something like this, using our name and likeness, without consulting any of us?"

They were in the dining room now and Gray had moved to stand near the fireplace. Dark oak columns stretched to the ceiling, guarding the old brick that surrounded the actual fire pit. The mantel was still there, even though it looked as if it had seen better days. Above hung a huge mirror, now marred with dust.

"I would think your father or someone from the network would have reached out to you and your siblings at some point," Morgan said, reminding him that he wasn't on this tour alone.

"Before his death, I hadn't spoken to my father since my high school graduation," Gray confessed.

He lifted a hand to run his fingers lightly along the dusty mantel. His thoughts traveled back to that day. They'd all gone to the same school, a public school because his mother hadn't wanted them to feel separated from the other children in town. Olivia never wanted her children to feel segregated or ostracized as she'd suspected they'd begun to feel while on the television show. The last time they'd seen their father before then was at their tenth birthday party, when Theodor also had business in the area. He'd dropped by their house just in time to sing "Happy Birthday" and drop off his gifts. Then he was gone. At the graduation he'd been there for the entire ceremony, telling each one of them how proud he was at the end, and then leaving again. That time he'd had a woman with him. Gray believed that was the moment his mother had truly become ill, even though she would live another four years before dying from complications of pneumonia.

"He didn't come around much after he left us," he continued.

"Why did he leave?"

Her voice was quiet, but close, as if she was standing right behind him. Gray didn't turn around to see, he simply took a deep breath before speaking words he'd never spoken before in his life.

"My father had an affair," he said solemnly. "It was with one of the production assistants on the show. My mother didn't find out, the way most clichéd cheating husbands meet their fate. No, my mother was oblivious. My sister Gemma used to say she was in love with her husband and her children, as if that was an excuse."

He paused, hearing the edge to his tone. "I don't blame her. In fact, I admire her for accepting and moving on the way she did. My father wanted to build a new life with this woman who had made her name from filming him and his family. So one night he told my mother he was leaving. The next morning, before my mother could even figure out what to do or say, he was gone. News spread like wildfire and many of the townspeople turned on my mom, blaming her for forcing the pregnancy and then having so many babies.

"It was a terrible time, that week following my dad's departure. My mother cried a lot. We stayed in the house with all the doors locked, the shades pulled down tight on the windows, as if we were being held hostage. There were lots of phone calls and arguments with the network executives. My mother didn't want to continue with the show. She hadn't wanted to do it after the first year anyway. The original plan had been to make enough money to start college funds for her children. But the demands of being in front of a camera nonstop and the subsequent promotion of the show were more than she wanted for herself or us. So she wanted out of the contract. If my father could get out of the marriage, then she felt like she could walk away from everything else. And she did."

"How old were you then?"

"Seven."

But Gray remembered feeling like he was a grown man with the amount of information he'd retained in that week alone. He'd heard the one-sided arguments as his mother spoke on the phone and stood outside the door of the sunroom while she'd talked to her grandfather. "She always sounded so strong when she talked of the plans for our new life. But I knew she cried at night. I heard her. We all did."

"That's so sad," Morgan whispered.

Gray turned then and saw that she was, in fact, standing right behind him. She hadn't turned on any lights in the room, but the old curtains were open at the windows and the lampposts right outside provided a hazy glow of illumination. She looked ethereal as she stood there, her gaze trained on his. Her hands were clasped in front of her and Gray knew that she was feeling the same disappointment he'd experienced as a young child.

"What makes you sad, Morgan?" Gray asked, even though he wasn't totally sure why.

Whenever he looked at her that happened. He found himself wanting to know more about her, needing to touch her, or to taste her once more. There was this tugging between him and her that had been there since that very first night and he was damned if he could explain it.

She licked her lips quickly and shook her head. "I try not to think of sad things," she replied.

"But it's inevitable, isn't it? Life happens and more often than not it brings sadness. I want to know what hurts you, so that I can never do those things."

Those words could not have sounded any more foreign to Gray than if he'd spoken them in another language. But he couldn't take them back now, nor did he want to.

"I—" she began and then paused. Her hands unclasped, arms coming up to cross over her chest. "I was sad when my parents moved away to Australia." She took a deep breath and let it out quickly. "I know it was a good opportunity for my father, and my mother, too—she'd never been anywhere but Temptation. But I wanted them to stay here with me. I was only in the tenth grade when they left me and Wendy with my grandmother. It hurt."

"But you got over it," Gray concluded for her. "Then you fell in love. Was that a feeling that made you happy? Did it make you forget the pain you'd felt when your parents left?"

He wanted—no, needed—to hear her answers to those questions. Maybe it was because he'd been going through his entire life trying to figure out if there was an ever after to the pain he'd felt and witnessed. His mother's heartbreak had been real and had lasted until she'd taken her last breath. One man had done that to her and Gray swore he'd never forgive his father for it.

"James was like a breath of fresh air," she said and Gray noted the light that entered her eyes.

"He was everything that every guy I'd ever met in Temptation was not. Worldly and ambitious and at the same time a gentleman. I didn't think about him romantically at first because I was just so amazed at the things he knew and the places he'd been. But then slowly that changed and just when I thought I couldn't love any one person any more, I had the twins."

She shook her head and looked out the window, then back to Gray. "There are no words to describe how I felt after giving birth. The only word to accurately depict how I felt with two-year-old babies, and the announcement that my husband was dead, would be *devastated*. That pain was just all consuming."

Just like Gray's mother had experienced when his father left. He gritted his teeth and turned away from her again. Placing his hands on the mantel, he dropped his head and tried to let those thoughts go. He was too old for this. All of the things that had happened to hurt him in the past were over and done with. He couldn't change them even if he'd tried. This was the present, he continued to tell himself. This was the house that needed to be sold so that he and his siblings could get on with their lives.

There was no other choice—no matter what Morgan did or said, Gray knew what he had to do.

Chapter 6

"The first Christmas after James's death, Wendy and I drove to the outlet mall. There was a Santa village there and Wendy thought the twins were old enough to see Santa in person for the first time and not be afraid. So we walked through the small village and I remember there were trellises covered with artificial snow-tipped garland. There were four or five of them that stretched the length of the walkway until they reached Santa's chair and the elves' station. At the center of each of the trellises was a bundle of mistletoe. Wendy had been the one to remind me of something our grandmother had always insisted we do during the holiday season. So I wished upon the mistletoe. Just one wish under each bunch that I repeated every time I stood beneath it. Then the babies saw Santa and they laughed happily, taking the most adorable picture ever. It was the most perfect day," Morgan said before sighing.

"Santa doesn't always bring you what you want," Gray said quietly.

Morgan nodded, trying to keep her fingers from fidgeting, they wanted to reach up and touch him so badly. He'd sounded so depleted when he talked of his family and what had happened to them. Since the moment she'd met him Morgan had been convinced he was an arrogant, narrow-minded rich guy, but as she got to know about his past, she'd seen there was more to him. Deep inside there was an agony that he struggled with, a past that he was both embarrassed and hurt by. She could relate to the pain, but only in the basic sense of loss. No way could she imagine what it was like for a seven-year-old to watch his family fall apart and to witness his mother's heart breaking until she died. It was one of the saddest stories she'd ever heard, which probably made her all kinds of naive and overly sensitive, but she didn't care at the moment.

"That's mostly true," she replied. "But that's when you grow up and learn that what you want is not always what's best for you. I wished that I could get over James and move on with my life, that I could not hurt anymore, not for another minute. It didn't happen. But I learned to live with it."

"Really?" he asked.

He then moved quicker than she'd anticipated and before she could stop him, he'd wrapped his arms around her waist and pushed her back against the wall. She gasped. The motion was so fast and so shocking. Not because his touch had sent instant heat soaring throughout her body and the proximity of his face to hers made her want more than she ever had in her life. At least, she was really trying to convince herself that wasn't the reason.

"What if I said I want you?" he asked, his breath fanning warmly over her face.

"For—for Christmas?" she asked and felt like a colossal idiot.

He didn't smile, but shook his head, his hands slipping

under her coat to rub along her back. "No. Right now. I want you, Morgan."

He moved again and Morgan saw his arm lifting. He was going to touch her. No, wait, he was already touching her. She should move. She should put lots of distance between them to keep whatever was about to happen from happening. But she didn't. She couldn't. His fingers grazed her jaw, came over her chin, then up to tap her bottom lip.

"You can't want me," she said, her body beginning to tremble even though it was the last thing she wanted to do.

"I can and I do," he told her, his other hand falling softly to her hip. "I want to take you right here against this wall. What does wishing on mistletoe tell you about that?"

She wanted to moan, but that wasn't an answer. Dammit, she couldn't think of any words and she certainly wasn't thinking about mistletoe at a time like this. Morgan tried to breathe in deeply and exhale slowly—a known relaxation technique that usually worked...but not this time. His scent permeated every pore of her body and she actually felt dizzy with arousal.

"Gray," she whispered and the tip of his finger touched her tongue.

His other hand went lower, gripping the curve of her bottom and pulling her up close to his arousal. He was thick and hard and she licked his finger, because what else was she supposed to do?

"Don't," he said. "Please, just don't deny this. There are so many things going on, I just need for this to be real. Whatever this is between us needs to be real and not some wish."

If a huge sprig of mistletoe was dangling over their heads right at this moment, Morgan knew exactly what she'd wish for. Now, whether or not that wish would come true...she didn't have another second to contemplate.

Gray's lips took the place of his finger as he kissed

her deeply. Her hands went to his shoulders, grabbing the leather of his jacket in a tight grip. He pressed closer as his tongue delved deeper into her mouth. The kiss was a scorcher, burning her from the tip of her tongue to the heels of her feet. She came up on tiptoes to meet him, and his hand continued to knead her bottom, until she finally lifted her leg and he wrapped it around his waist. Morgan finally gave in to the moan as he devoured her mouth and she accepted every delicious stroke of his tongue. The room was spinning, a kaleidoscope of lights pouring into the dark space. Heat surrounded them even though the furnace in the house was not lit.

Gray thrust his hips into her and Morgan trembled in his arms. The feel of his arousal pressed against her center had her quaking with need, even though the connection was hampered by their clothes.

"Now," he whispered. "I need you now."

Her body screamed yes. Her nipples were so hard pressing against his chest it was almost painful. How long had it been? Morgan had actually forgotten. The need was so great, her hunger so potent it almost choked her. Yes. Just say it, she told herself. Say it and let go.

"Stop," she whispered. "Please stop."

He did, immediately.

Morgan pulled away from him, breathing heavily as she made her way out of the dining room and back through the house the way they'd come. She was running, she knew, but didn't give a damn. He'd scared her. The need that was so great inside her for him was terrifying. It had surpassed anything Morgan had ever felt before, for anyone. Even James.

Digging into her jacket pocket, she fumbled for her keys as she ran down the front steps of the house and over the lawn until she reached the spot where she'd parked her car. Finally unlocking the door, without looking back or caring where Gray was, she jumped inside and put the key in the ignition. Turning it, she called herself every type of idiot in the book, but prayed just to get home. She would get her kids, put them to bed and then find herself a glass… no, a bottle of wine to drink. Completely. It was going to be that kind of night, she thought as she turned the key in the ignition again, and waited.

Nothing.

The engine didn't turn over. In fact, it didn't make a sound. Cursing, Morgan tried again, and then once more, before she finally slapped her palms on the steering wheel.

She jumped at the knock on her window and closed her eyes to the sight of Gray standing there.

"Is there a mechanic's shop around here?" Gray asked after they'd driven in silence for more than five minutes.

She hadn't wanted to get into his car. In fact, she'd gone as far as pulling out her cell phone and attempting to call her sister to come and pick her up. But her sister did not answer, which had only irritated her more as the children were supposed to be with Wendy at their grandmother's house. She'd said as much in between ranting about her car being undependable. When he'd finally heard enough, Gray had simply led her to his car, opened the door and had been about to ease her inside when she looked at him with a serious glare.

"I can take care of myself," she'd stated.

"But can you fix your car?" he'd asked.

When she didn't reply, but simply slipped inside the car and stared straight ahead, Gray had counted it as a victory. She could have replied yes and he would have been more defeated than shocked. He absolutely believed that this woman could do anything she put her mind to. Still, there was no doubt that Morgan Hill was one stubborn woman.

"Yes," she finally said in response to his current question.

Gray noticed how far she'd moved in her seat. It was a good thing he'd made sure the passenger side door was locked, or she may have fallen out as he drove.

"If you know the name of the place I can call them while you run in and get your kids," he told her when he turned down the street where her grandmother lived.

"That's not necessary," she told him. "I can call in the morning."

Gray nodded, having momentarily forgotten where he was. In Miami and most major cities, he guessed, leaving a car abandoned was like an invitation for vandals, the car to be stolen or towed. But this was Temptation, and while she was parked in front of an empty house and people would definitely notice her car there in the morning, Gray doubted anyone would bother it. They were probably more likely to call her and ask her why she'd left it parked there, or worse, come up with their own reason and spread it throughout the town. Just as someone had obviously done when he'd returned.

"I was just thinking about your car possibly being stolen, but I guess that's not an issue here," he told her.

"No," she said when he pulled into the driveway. "We don't do that here."

As soon as he stopped the car, she pushed the button to unlock her door and opened it to get out. Gray reached out and touched her arm.

"I'm just trying to help, Morgan. I'm sorry if what happened back there made you uncomfortable."

She pulled her arm slowly from his grasp. "I'm not uncomfortable," she said. "At least not the way you think. I mean…" She sighed and then turned to face him.

"I'll get Wendy to take me home."

"That's ridiculous. I'm here, just go get your kids and I'll drive you home."

"I don't want to impose and I don't want…whatever

this is…or what you think you might be doing with me. It's just not going to work and I don't want to give you the wrong idea," she told him.

Gray was just about to tell her that it wasn't her. It was totally him. He couldn't take back the kiss, nor did he want to. Still, he knew the moment she'd pulled away from him that she'd regretted it.

"Who's that?" an older woman's voice asked outside the car, just before she began tapping on the windshield.

"Who is this coming to my house unannounced? You better not be selling anything!" the woman continued.

Gray could see her using a cane to tap on the window again. She either didn't know the act could break the glass, or simply didn't care.

"I'll call the sheriff and…wait a minute, Morgan? Is that you?" the woman asked.

Morgan simply shook her head and stepped out of the car. "Yes, it's me, Granny."

This was her grandmother.

Gray opened his door gingerly. The older woman was leaning over his side of the car. She backed up a little, still holding her cane out in front of her like a weapon. She was a little taller than Morgan, with a slimmer frame. It was dark, but the motion lights affixed to the top of the garage had come on so Gray could see the woman's very light complexion. Her glasses were large framed and black, her gray hair pulled back from her face.

"Ida Mae Bonet, meet Grayson Taylor," Morgan said as she'd come to stand beside the woman. "Gray, this is my grandmother."

Gray immediately stepped forward and extended his hand. "It's a pleasure to meet you, ma'am," he said.

She grabbed his hand, pulling him closer as she looked up at him. That must not have been good enough because then she hooked her cane on her other arm and used her free hand to pull her glasses down her nose so she could look over them.

"Hot damn! You sure are Grayson. The oldest boy. You used to wet the bed, too. Olivia didn't know what to do about that. I told her to put a hand to your bottom and you'd stop that nonsense," she said before laughing like she'd told the best joke ever.

If she wasn't still holding tight to Gray's arm, he may have tried to leave at that moment. Embarrassment didn't even seem to describe what he was feeling at this moment.

"Granny, where are the children?" Morgan asked as if she sensed Gray's discomfort.

"Oh, they're in the house fast asleep. I made my famous beef stew tonight. Let them run around and play until the bread finished baking, then I fed 'em. Before I could get the dishes washed they were asleep," Ida Mae said.

"It's not quite their bedtime, but I guess that's okay. I'll just go on inside and Wendy can take us home."

"Oh, she's not here," Ida Mae said quickly, stopping Morgan from walking away.

"What do you mean she's not here? She said they were going to get pizza and watch movies while I was meeting with Gray at the Taylor house," Morgan insisted.

Ida Mae shook her head, looking up to Gray once more. "You went back home, did ya? How'd you like that?"

"Granny, where's Wendy?" Morgan interrupted, clearly not interested in Gray's feelings on his family home at the moment.

That was just fine with Gray.

"Oh, she had to go in to work," Ida Mae said, waving a hand at her granddaughter. "Let's all go in and you both can get the babies. I'll bet Grayson has room in this shiny little car to fit them. He can take you home. That's what a gentleman would do after a date," she said and hooked her arm in Gray's.

He smiled. It came naturally to him, without having to think or wonder if it was the right thing to do. In the last two days, two women had linked their arm in his. In his entire life he had lost count of how many other women had done this. But none of them compared one bit to these women in Temptation.

Gray tried not to pay attention to the look of frustration on Morgan's face as he and Ida Mae moved into the house.

Old colonial was the style of Ida Mae's house, and Gray got a homey and welcoming feeling the second he was inside. The floors were covered in dark brown carpet and the walls had pictures of family members, no doubt. Some were old, in black and white, while others were in color and most likely more recent. There was furniture everywhere, which was a contrast to his more minimal decor back in Miami. A sofa, love seat and two recliners filled the living room. There was a coffee table with magazines neatly stacked, end tables with lamps, ashtrays and pictures in frames. Across the back of the sofa was a colorful quilt that looked old and precious. When he inhaled, he smelled the faint scent of Ida Mae's beef stew and homemade bread.

"They're lying back here in the den," Ida Mae said as she continued walking through the living room and into a smaller room. In the adjoining room there was a big-screen television that looked totally out of place with another old sofa and rocking chair across from it.

"Little darlins, aren't they?" Ida Mae asked Gray when he entered the room behind her.

"Yes," he replied because he wasn't certain what else to say.

Gray also wasn't sure what was going on. How did he end up in this house, which distinctly reminded him of his grandfather's house—the one he'd had here in Temptation before he'd died? And why was he thinking of the Sunday dinners his mother used to cook for them, the ones that she made them get dressed up for and had used her best dishes to set the table?

"They won't have their booster seats in your car, but I guess it'll be okay this one time. If you could just take Jack to the car, I'll get Lily," Morgan said as she moved past him. "I really appreciate your offer to take us home, Gray."

She did appreciate it, Gray thought. But she definitely did not like it.

He picked up Jack and the little boy instantly wrapped his arms around Gray's neck.

"Kids know," Ida Mae said, looking at Gray with a smile. "They know before grown folk do."

Gray didn't wait to hear an explanation and instead said a quick good-night as Morgan headed for the door. She'd yelled back to her grandmother that she'd call her in the morning, but Ida Mae was still talking to Gray as she walked with him to the door.

"Your mother was a strong woman. She did what was best for her children. That's what a good woman does. And a good man, well, he walks his own path," she said.

Gray turned to her then and said what came first to his mind. "I'm not like my father."

Ida Mae stared at him for a few moments before nodding. "You know, I don't think you are. Nope, I sure don't think you are."

He thought about Ida's words as he drove down more quiet streets. The houses were not equally spread apart and did not look the same, but all had a quaintness that Gray didn't see in Miami. He tried to ignore that, too. Morgan was quiet. Gray suspected she was trying to ignore him. He figured that made them two of a kind.

Her house was long, almost like a trailer, but Gray knew it was one of those prefab homes. He'd seen a few in Miami and had once entertained the idea of investing in a company that specialized in them. He had thought that the dwellings didn't feel like real houses. But when he walked into Morgan's, he felt differently. This was her home.

It was neat, with a homey feel. There was a corner full of the children's toys in the small living room. Going back farther there was a neat table that seated four and beyond that was a kitchen with cheery yellow paint. The bedrooms were past a bathroom and what Gray thought might be a closet. There were only two. The one to the left belonged to the children. The one to the right, he deduced, was Morgan's bedroom.

"Jack's bed is over there," she told him as she entered the room.

She hadn't turned on the light but the one in the hallway partially lit the room. Gray moved to the bed and laid Jack down easily. He looked over his shoulder and saw that Morgan was slipping off Lily's shoes. He did the same with Jack.

Gray stared down at the sleeping boy and felt something shift inside. Jack was a good-looking kid. His complexion was just a shade lighter than his mother's creamy brown. His hair was darker, his eyebrows thick, lips partially open as he slept.

"Thank you," he heard Morgan say from behind.

Gray turned to her. "You're welcome."

They stood there, staring at each other for what felt like a lifetime, before Morgan moved.

"I'll walk you out," she said after closing the bedroom door.

Yes, he should leave, Gray thought as he followed her. He should leave this house because he couldn't stop himself from wanting to ask how she liked living there alone with her kids. When he was at her grandmother's he'd wanted to know if they had Sunday dinners there. Morgan, the twins, her sister and Ida Mae. Did they spend Christmas Eve together and wake up on Christmas morning to a huge tree and lots of gifts? How did the children react? Did they try to defy sleep and wait for Santa? What was on their Christmas list this year?

No, he shook his head as he came closer to her front door. Those weren't questions he needed answers to. That wasn't why he was here.

"About earlier," Morgan began.

Her back was to him as she let one hand rest on the doorknob.

Gray cleared his throat and tried to do the same with his mind. She'd taken off her jacket and he could now see that the shirt she wore was fitted to her compact body. His hands itched to touch her pert breasts, his body heating with each breath he took because it was full of her scent.

What the hell was wrong with him?

"What about it?" he asked gruffly.

"I don't know why it happened," she told him as she turned to face him. "I—I mean, not since my husband." She cleared her throat this time. "I'm not that type of woman. I don't sleep with guys I've just met. I don't sleep around. Sex is not casual for me. I just—"

"You just want me as badly as I want you, that's all," he said and removed his jacket.

"If you're asking yourself why, I don't know the answer." Gray tossed his coat to the floor and immediately began undoing the buttons of his shirt. Her gaze followed his movements but she did not speak.

"I didn't come here for this," he said, a part of him still feeling totally confused.

Her children weren't that far away. Sure they were asleep and they'd closed the bedroom door, but she had children. That fact alone should have curtailed his actions, but they did not. He undid the belt and buckle of his pants.

"But just like in business I know when to act and when to retreat," he told her, his hand resting over his erection.

She licked her lips and Gray thought he would come right then and there.

"This isn't business," she whispered.

"No," he told her before lifting a hand to crook a finger at her, beckoning her to come closer. "This is definitely not business."

Chapter 7

She wasn't going to stop him.

Even though her children weren't that far away. They were asleep in their bedroom and rarely ever woke during the night.

No, she wasn't going to stop him, or this.

It was an impulsive decision and that was not her style. This was more like something Wendy would do. Taking a chance, walking on the wild side. When had her normally cautious demeanor changed? Maybe it was when she'd taken that first step toward him. Or, perhaps it was the second his strong hands grabbed hold of her shirt, yanking it out of her pants, up and over her head without saying a word. It could have been the moment his gaze dropped to her breasts and rested there.

It didn't really matter because the sigh she'd just released was one of total surrender.

He'd carried her over to the couch, lifting her right off her feet in one swift motion. When he laid her down it was with a gentleness that she hadn't expected. Her body hummed with desire, her hands shaking with the urge to reach out and touch him. His shirt hung on his shoulders, the white tank he wore beneath melded to his chest and abs. She wanted him naked. That was the first thought she had as she lay back on the couch.

She'd turned on a lamp across the room when they had come in, so there was a soft golden glow around them. He looked like a bronzed god as he seemed to read her mind and stripped off his shirt and tank top. He looked like a bodybuilder, she thought. Or a professional athlete of some sort. Morgan knew Gray looked good in a suit. That's all she'd ever seen him in. But she had no idea that without clothes he would be this...gorgeous.

When she sat up and lifted a hand to him, he stepped closer and allowed her to push his pants over his hips. She was shaking, Morgan thought as her hands clumsily moved over the bulge in his boxers. It had been so long. He cupped her face in his hands then, tilting her head until she looked up at him. He didn't speak and Morgan didn't really think he needed to. She knew what he wanted, because it was what she wanted, too.

She let her hands fall from him and slipped them behind her back to unclasp her bra. He took off his shoes. She unbuttoned her jeans and pushed them down her legs until she realized they weren't going to move past her ankle boots. He unzipped the boots and slipped them from her feet. She then pushed her pants off completely. He had already stepped out of his pants and was now rubbing one hand from her ankle up to her thigh. His touch was soft and tantalizing. It was a simple one and yet undeniably sexy as tendrils of desire shot through her body. He stroked her other leg, spreading them apart slightly, and Morgan gasped. He cupped a hand over her juncture and she felt her arousal seeping through the cotton material of her panties. For a second she thought that perhaps she should be embarrassed that she wasn't wearing something sexier. The look of pure pleasure on Gray's face when his gaze locked on hers had that feeling dissipating. Her panties were removed next before Gray came over her, his lips immediately finding hers.

Again his kiss was hungry, hot and everything she'd come to expect from him. Her hands rubbed along his strong back, her legs wrapping around his waist. The first touch of his hot length against her damp center sent another spike of lust vibrating through her. She jumped and gasped and he whispered in her ear, "I've got you, baby."

Morgan liked the sound of his voice. He'd called her *baby* and she'd shivered. He kissed along the line of her jaw and she trembled.

"You don't understand," she said, but he didn't stop kissing her.

She was drowning in his kiss, her hardened nipples rubbing against his broad chest.

"It's been a while," she whispered and flattened her hands against his chest. "I mean, um, not since…"

Gray touched a finger to her lips to silence her.

"I understand," he said softly. "Are you sure you want to do this?"

His gaze seemed a bit softer, although his eyes were still darkened by desire. His jaw was strong as she lifted shaking fingers to touch him. There were so many reasons for her to answer no and only one for her to say yes. Morgan had suspected that it had been hard for a man like Grayson Taylor to refrain from anything he wanted. His wants and needs were always met, probably without him ever having to voice them. Yet he had with her.

"I want you," she told him without wavering another moment. "I want you, Gray."

She was the one to lift up at that moment, at the same

time guiding his head down so that their mouths could meet for a kiss. Their tongues dueled, moans mingled, and Gray slowly slipped inside of her. There was a rush of heat, a slight tensing, and then Morgan was falling. She matched Gray's thrusts, her eyes closing involuntarily as she held tight to him for fear of falling off the cliff to a bottomless abyss.

Every stroke, every whisper, every time he kissed her shoulder, her chin, her closed lids and her lips—it was all intoxicating. Morgan forgot everything and everyone. There was only Gray. Only this moment and he filled it and her with complete satisfaction.

So complete that she didn't want it to end.

Yet, she knew that it would. It had to, and then where would she be?

He held her when she trembled in his arms, her release taking her completely by surprise. It was a wave of pleasure that she couldn't resist but wanted to hold on to for dear life. Gray fell right behind her, holding her so tightly she could barely breathe. It was a wonderful feeling, a safe and cherished feeling, which, of course, Morgan knew would end and probably too soon.

"What are you doing here?"

"I'm picking you up for work. You do have to teach today, right?" Gray said the next morning when he showed up at her door.

Morgan didn't understand. Well, she did, but she hadn't anticipated that he'd be there. She'd already talked to Wendy—who was apologetic about last night—this morning. Her sister was supposed to roll out of bed and bring Morgan her car to use today. When she got to work she planned to call Otis to see if he could tow her car over to Smitty's, Temptation's only official auto-mechanic shop. She had not expected to see Gray at all.

"There's no need to inconvenience your sister. I'm here and I can take you," he insisted.

"You were here last night," Jack said.

Morgan had left Jack and Lily at the kitchen table with orders to finish their cereal while she answered the door. Apparently, Jack was finished. Morgan doubted that, but here he was.

"Yes, I was, and you were sound asleep," Gray replied.

"Not all the way. Your car has cold seats," Jack continued and Morgan froze.

She wondered if Jack remembered anything else about last night besides riding in Gray's car. Her son hadn't mentioned anything about Gray this morning, so the fact that he knew he'd been here was news to her. Yet another thing for her to think carefully about today.

Gray gave a nod as he moved past Morgan and into the living room. "I have seat warmers. We can turn those on this morning. I think it's colder today."

"It's gonna snow," Jack told him.

Morgan closed and locked the door behind her, turning in time to see Gray and Jack walking back toward the kitchen like they were old friends. They weren't, however. Gray was just passing through town. He would be gone as soon as he decided what to do with his buildings. Then they would never see him again. He'd made it perfectly clear that he did not like being back in Temptation. The pain, for him, was too great, and Morgan could understand that. No matter how her body wanted something totally different.

"Mr. Gray!" she heard Lily chime just before she entered the kitchen.

By the time she entered, she saw Lily once again in Gray's arms. Jack, who was standing close to his leg, looked up as he asked, "Do you know how to build a snowman?"

Gray had been touching the ends of Lily's hair. Her

daughter had wanted to have the ends of her ponytails left loose today. No twists or bows at the end, she'd instructed Morgan. Normally, Morgan didn't like for Lily's long and sometimes untamable hair to be worn loose while she was in school. It made for a distraction that the ABCs could not compete with. This morning, however, the conflict over just how wrong Morgan had been to have sex with a guy she hardly knew, on the couch in her living room, while her children were in the other room fast asleep, had made her a little more relaxed on the rules.

"I haven't seen snow in a very long time," Gray told Jack.

"How can you not see snow? It comes every year," Jack insisted, his little brow furrowed in confusion.

"We have fifteen minutes, you two. Finish your breakfast," Morgan interjected. "Would you like a cup of coffee?" she offered Gray, since he was there.

"Sure," he replied, sitting Lily down in her chair.

Jack slipped into his seat and scooped another spoon of cereal into his mouth, drops of milk dripping down his chin. Morgan looked up after taking another mug down from the cabinet to see Gray leaning in to wipe Jack's face with one of the napkins from the center of the table.

"How do you like it?" she asked, her voice unusually loud.

Gray and the children looked her way.

"Your coffee, I mean," she clarified, feeling uncomfortable.

The scene before her was extremely domestic and she didn't know how to digest it. Just like in her dining room, there was just a small table in the center of the kitchen floor where, normally, only three people sat. None of those people had been a man, because there had been no male in her life since James.

"Black," Gray replied.

James liked lots of cream and sugar in his coffee, just like Morgan did. Her husband hadn't been a millionaire, either. He'd driven a Jeep and not a Porsche. He was exactly six feet tall, not an inch over. Gray was much taller and more muscular than James. She wouldn't say Gray was stronger or more handsome, though. She just couldn't. It would be disrespectful to James's memory. Hell, everything she'd done and thought since meeting Grayson Taylor had been like spitting on all the love and memories she'd shared with James Hill and Morgan hated that thought.

"I live in Miami," Gray informed the children. "We don't get snow to build snowmen."

"No snowmen?" Lily asked. "That's sad. I want it to snow on Christmas. Just like the song Mama listens to on the radio."

"She listens to those songs all the time," Jack quipped.

"All right you two, less talking and more eating," Morgan chided lightly as she brought Gray's coffee to the table.

There was nothing else for her to do but take a seat across from Gray while the children continued to eat.

"Mr. Taylor's going to give us a ride this morning," she announced when there had been a few moments of silence while the children finally did what she'd told them to do. Her cell phone was sitting on the table and she picked it up to send Wendy a text to let her know.

"Where's your car?" Lily asked.

"It died." Jack shook his head. "Just like our dad. Did you know that our dad died, Mr. Taylor?"

Morgan almost dropped the mug she'd just been bringing to her lips. Her gaze shot to Gray's, but he only looked mildly taken aback. He probably wasn't used to the candor of children. Morgan was, but she had to admit that she hadn't anticipated Jack bringing up his father. The children rarely said anything about James, because they had no real memories of him, aside from the things that Morgan had told them.

Gray had just taken a sip from his coffee and now he slowly lowered his mug to the table as he looked from Morgan to Jack.

"My father died, too. Just over two months ago," Gray told him.

"Did he get shot?" Lily asked.

"Maybe we shouldn't be talking about this right now," Morgan said trying to intercede.

Gray shook his head as he looked over to her and said, "It's fine."

It wasn't, Morgan wanted to yell, but she didn't want to argue in front of the children.

"No. He wasn't shot," Gray said to Lily. "He had a heart attack."

"Oh," Lily said, her eyes wide now. "Our dad was in the army."

"He was a soldier," Jack offered. "He was fighting wars to help people but he got shot instead."

Morgan's chest constricted at the words and her hands shook so she pulled them away from the mug completely. Her mind was whirling with guilty thoughts about James and having this man sitting here at the table with James's children. A part of her knew how silly that was. James would never have expected her to remain a widow for the rest of her life. He would have wished for her to find happiness again, even if that happiness was in the arms of another man.

But Gray wasn't that man. There was no happiness to be found with him because he had no plans to stay in Temptation. Not to mention the fact that Morgan wasn't the type of woman that landed a man like Grayson Taylor. She knew that each time she let herself recall meeting Kym Hutchins. That woman—as much as Morgan instinctively did not like her—was exactly the type that would be on Gray's arm.

"It's time to go," Morgan said as she immediately stood. "Grab your coats while I clear the table."

The children were glad to be finished with their breakfast and hurriedly pushed away from the table. They were on their way out of the room when Jack turned back and asked Gray, "Are you going to heat up the seats now?"

Gray nodded. "Sure will. By the time you come outside they'll be all warm for you."

Jack smiled. "Okay, I'll hurry."

Now alone, Morgan struggled for the right words. She would text Wendy and cancel, then she would accept Gray's ride to work this morning, only because he was already here and they were in danger of being late. But then she wanted him to stay away from her children.

"You look like there's a battle going on inside your head," she heard him say.

"What?" she asked and picked up the two bowls from the table, then carried them to the sink.

"Your brow's all wrinkled and you were rubbing the back of your neck like you were trying to push some difficult thoughts out of your mind," he told her.

Morgan put the bowls in the sink and tried to relax. He was right, but he didn't need to know that. "I'd like my car to be fixed and I'm hoping that Otis can get to it today."

"Otis? He's the guy at the B and B?"

"Yes," she answered. "He does a lot of odd jobs around town since his wife died. Before that he'd worked at the train station for thirty-five years and then retired. Granny says he used to drive Ms. Ethel crazy when he was sitting in that house all day doing nothing. Now he spends his days helping out at the B and B and wandering around town giving people rides, dropping off packages, fixing broken bikes or raking up the leaves. Anything to keep him from sitting still too long because then he'd miss Ethel too much."

She'd said the last quietly, her hands clenching the side of the sink.

"Like you miss your husband?" Gray asked softly.

Morgan turned quickly and was shocked to see that he'd gotten up from the table and now stood just a couple feet away from her.

"I—I didn't say anything about that. About him, I mean," she said and then paused. Taking a deep breath, Morgan let it out slowly. "I apologize for the children bringing him up. I don't know where that conversation came from."

Gray looked as if he was going to say something, then he stopped and simply waited.

"I can't do this," she admitted. "I don't know how to do this casual sleep-together thing that I'm sure you're used to. I'm not as worldly as you or Kym and I don't want to be. All I ever wanted was to have a family and to live right here in Temptation, just like my parents did. I never expected my husband to die so quickly and now I can only focus on my kids. I hope you don't sell those buildings because they mean a lot to us. Your father even had plans for them. Although I'm not sure they were the best plans. Still, the town's counting on you continuing with your father's ideas so that we can reap the revenue and hopefully draw in more tourists. There are lots of updates we need here in Temptation. We could be such a rich and prosperous town for future generations, but if you sell, outsiders will come in and do what they want."

She stopped because she'd been babbling. All the things that had been rolling through her mind for many nights just came tumbling out and now her heart pounded and her hands shook.

Gray took a step toward her. He reached out, cupping

a hand at the nape of her neck. He didn't rub the spot, but simply held his hand still there. The heat and comfort spread instantaneously and she almost leaned into him with relief.

"I'm not trying to make you forget your husband," he said quietly. "I don't know what a love that deep feels like, but I have to say it's admirable. As for the town, I don't know what I'm going to do about that yet."

It was an honest answer, she figured. Honest and conflicted. Was Gray having as hard a time dealing with his dead father as she was with the strong memory of her dead husband?

"Now, let's get you to work," he said, pulling his hand slowly away from her. "You don't want to be late."

He'd walked out of the kitchen then, leaving Morgan alone with her thoughts. The ones that did not want to obey her declarations. She did feel guilty about James and she did want what was best for the town. But she also wanted Grayson Taylor. Damn, how she wanted him.

Chapter 8

"I want all of his files delivered here. No later than to-morrow, Phil," Gray said into his cell phone. "And see if you can locate my brother Garrek."

After hanging up with his lawyer, Gray sat back in the chair at the coffee shop where he'd been for the last hour. The manager of the shop, a very lovely lady in her mid-forties named Clarice, had given him permission to use the back two tables as his makeshift office.

"I don't know why Jim and Darlene won't get with the times and have Wi-Fi installed out at the farm. I swear some people are so resistant to change," Clarice had told him as she'd brought him coffee and the whole wheat bagel he'd ordered.

"It's all right," he'd told her. "I kind of like the solitude, for small stretches of time, that is."

Gray smiled and for the first time since he'd been in Temptation, he felt totally relaxed.

After dropping Morgan and the children off at school

he'd come straight to the coffee shop with his tablet, cell phone and a small file he'd begun to compile late last night. He'd spent hours thinking about the time he'd spent at the old house. The feelings he'd felt while walking through the rooms, the memories that continued to push further and further to the forefront of his mind. They all swirled through his head until he'd spent most of the night and early morning sitting up staring out the window to the dark outline of the mountaintop. After finally getting a couple hours' sleep, he'd showered and headed straight to Morgan's house. There'd been no question that he'd drive her to work that morning.

With that done, now Gray had a lot of research he wanted to get done.

Theodor Taylor had been up to something before he'd died and Gray wanted to know what.

The man who he and his siblings had all developed a love-hate relationship with over the years had secrets. Gray had never doubted that. One of the things his mother had always said about their father was that he had an uncanny ability to keep things to himself, whereas she was an open book. Olivia had always blamed herself for that flaw. Gray had actually found it refreshing that all he'd ever had to do was ask his mother a question to get an honest answer.

Where his father was concerned, well, there weren't many times Gray had even attempted to ask the man anything of substance. During his childhood there had only been a couple of visits from his father and sporadic phone calls. Theodor just sent money. That was all he'd been able to do for his family after they left Temptation. Gray considered that enough since the man's presence never failed to upset his mother. Had he been left to make the choice about leaving town, he would have chosen to see his mother with some semblance of happiness every time.

Some of his other siblings didn't agree, but Gray couldn't carry their burdens as well as his own.

Morgan had told him that just about a year ago his father had been in touch with Fred Randall, the real estate agent and property manager. He was also Millie's husband. Gray had written all these names down last night. Now he typed the agent's name into the computer to see what he'd come up with. There wasn't much, but the agency did have a website with Fred and his wife smiling on the front page. They stood in front of a sparkling white colonial that Gray figured was their house. He went to the contacts page on the site and wrote down the address and phone number. He would pay Fred Randall a visit today.

"There you are," a female voice said as she approached the table. "I've been looking all over for you. Those people at that so-called resort you're staying at are rude and unprofessional. I guess I shouldn't expect too much considering where we are."

Gray looked up from his tablet to see Kym. "Good morning," he said to hopefully stop her from talking.

She sighed in return. "It will be when I get a decent cup of coffee. I swear, one of the first things I'm going to do when I get back to the office is write a letter to Starbucks and tell them they need to open up a shop in this ho-hum town."

"Ms. Clarice makes a wonderful latte," Gray told her as he resumed shutting down all the windows he'd opened on his screen. He'd closed the document he'd been writing the moment Kym sat down.

"I don't want a latte," she told him. "I want an extra-hot grande caramel macchiato with extra caramel and I don't need anybody asking me if I'm going caroling tonight, either."

Caroling was tonight, Gray thought as he sat back in his chair. Clarice had told him about it when he'd first come in. She said they'd start at city hall and walk down Main Street so that all the shoppers could hear them as they mulled about in the local stores.

"Joya and Martina will have hot cocoa and hot soups at the church afterward," Clarice had added with a wide grin. "You ain't had nothing 'til you've tasted Joya's Maryland crab soup."

Gray had nodded and thanked her for telling him, but until this moment when Kym mentioned it, he hadn't given much thought to attending. Now, he found himself wondering if Morgan would want to go with the children. Not as disturbed by that thought as he should have been, Gray reluctantly returned his attention to Kym.

"Did you bring the contracts for me to sign?" he asked her, already knowing what her answer would be.

She shook her head, then frowned as the young waitress—instead of Clarice—brought Kym her cup of coffee. When the woman walked away, Kym leaned over to sniff the beverage and rolled her eyes.

"No. I don't have the contracts and obviously I don't have a good cup of coffee, either," she snapped.

"I'd really like to get those contracts signed, Kym, since you've come all this way. Then you can make arrangements to head back to the office," he told her.

"When are you coming back to the office?" she asked.

She was wearing beige pants and a jacket with a peach turtleneck today. Her hair was pulled back neatly, gold earrings at her ears. She looked crisp and efficient, a bit rigid and way too attitudinal. Gray had never made that assessment of her before.

"There's more to work here than I originally thought," he told her. "So I'm going to stay a little longer."

Last night, before he'd put Jack to bed, and before he'd had sex with Jack's mother on their couch, Gray only thought he'd stay in Temptation for a few more days while he figured out what exactly his father had planned. This morning when he'd heard the children speak of their father and saw the pain of losing her husband still so clear in Morgan's eyes, he'd decided to work through his business a little quicker. He figured he'd need another day or two just to get all the facts straight in his mind. That's how Gray liked to make decisions—with all the facts and a thorough list of pros and cons before him. There had never been memories or emotions in the mix. Hence the reason he hadn't been able to give Kym the exact timeline of his return.

"Then I'll stay and help you," she immediately offered. "What do you need? I can pull the numbers on property taxes and values in this area. We can also do a study on the town's viability as a tourist destination and historical landmark. While I was wandering around with nothing to do last night, I heard from many of the townspeople about all the battles fought in Temptation. Some of them were also talking about an outlet mall possibly being built here to help bolster their economy. There were two women in particular who had more details than the others. I told them that would be a wonderful idea. That's exactly what they need here, a blast of the twenty-first century."

"A mall? Where would they put an outlet mall?" Gray asked, his attention now firmly back on the town and what his father's plans were.

"The first woman said something about the land behind the community center was the prime location. I don't know where a community center is here, but she seemed hopeful. The other woman—I didn't get either of their names, but she was the loud and bossy one, with a bad highlight job—interrupted, declaring the community center was vital to the town and should stay where it is." Kym shook her head. "Old people hate progress."

"Progress shouldn't always entail forgetting the past," he said thoughtfully.

Gray wasn't totally sure where those words had come from, or why he'd felt the need to say them. The look Kym gave him said she couldn't believe he'd said them, either.

"You do know our business is about future innovation," she said, her brows lifted in question. "I mean, that's what we do at Gray Technologies. We're constantly trying to stay three steps ahead of anyone else. Developing the most high-tech and revolutionary ideas around. If you have the chance, why wouldn't you wish the same for the town where you were born?"

He didn't have an immediate answer. That did not deter Kym. In fact, Gray thought as he watched her lean forward, a familiar gleam appearing in her eyes, she already had something specific in mind.

"What we should do is find out who the developer is for the outlet mall. We can meet with him and secure its biggest lot for the Gray Café. Think of all the publicity behind Grayson Taylor returning to his hometown to open the first brick-and-mortar Gray Technologies store. It would be phenomenal! And most of the publicity would be free. The town would probably foot the bill since this will definitely increase their revenue," she said, her excitement evident.

Gray frowned. Maybe because Millie Randall and Otis had just walked through the front door and the first thing Otis said was his name.

"Damned if I didn't talk the city slicker up," Otis said as he begin making his way back to where Gray and Kym were sitting.

"Mornin', ma'am. You're looking pretty as a picture today," Otis said, pulling a worn herringbone cap from his head as he made a mock bow in front of Kym.

She didn't scowl, but the smile she gave him was less than enthusiastic. "Good morning," she said.

"Mornin' to you, son," Otis said when he was once again standing as straight as he could and looking over to Gray. "You keeping this woman busy with all your work and stuff? She needs time to get out and see the sights. Maybe she wants to go caroling tonight? If not, couple of us grown folk will be down at Pat's Bar. Nothing like hot chocolate with a dash of tequila."

Gray almost chuckled. He totally believed this man would have a bottle of tequila sitting right beside his mug of hot chocolate.

"I don't think we'll be stopping by the bar tonight," Gray told him.

"But you should come out for the caroling," Millie added as she joined them.

"Hello, Ms. Millie," Gray said. "Let me introduce you to my assistant, Kym."

Millie was already shaking her head, heavy gold-and-orange earrings moving at her ears. "We already met last night," Millie informed Gray without giving Kym a glance.

"You were out with Morgan last night, right? How did you like seeing your old home? Olivia and Theodor were so happy there," she continued.

Gray gritted his teeth at that presumption, then decided it was better to be cordial to Millie, especially since he would need to speak with her husband regarding his father's dealings in the last year. Besides, it wasn't her fault that his father had fooled the citizens of this town.

He was just about to respond when he noticed Kym staring at him. It was a look that he wondered if he should address. He didn't, of course. There were too many ears around. He did, however, try to reroute the conversation.

"Ms. Millie, if you could let your husband know that I'd like to stop by his office this afternoon to speak to him about the properties and my father, I would really appreciate it," he told her.

Millie smiled and nodded. "Of course, I'll give him a call right now." She began fumbling through a purse that looked more like a piece of carry-on luggage.

"You going down to the real estate office?" Otis asked.

"Yes. I have a few calls to make right now so I'm going to head back to my room. But I'll be back in town a little later this afternoon so I can see Mr. Randall then."

Otis began scratching his head. He looked as if he was trying to figure something out, but Gray had no idea what.

"Oh, I just thought you'd be heading over to the school this afternoon. You know, to pick up Morgan and the kids. Heard you dropped them off this morning," Otis said.

Kym put down the cup she was sipping from with a loud clanking sound. Not only did Gray look her way, but Otis and Millie did also.

"I thought her car would be fixed by now," Gray replied when he turned back to face Otis. "She said she was going to have it towed."

Otis nodded. "Yep. I got right over there this morning after she called me. Got it all hitched up to the back of my truck and took it down to Smitty's. He owns the garage, you know. But Smitty said he's got to order some part, seeing as the car's so old it might be a while before it comes in."

"Oh, it's going to be brisk this afternoon," Millie chimed in, obviously putting off the phone call to her husband. "I told Georgia down at the church to make sure there was plenty of blankets and hot chocolate for tonight because people are going to be downright chilled to the bone when they come in. Those kids shouldn't be walking home in this weather," she said with a knowing nod to Gray.

"No," he said. "They shouldn't."

"We were going to meet with the real estate man this afternoon, correct, Gray? Are you going to call your husband and confirm his availability?" Kym asked Millie.

Millie not only ignored Kym's question, but she also turned so that her back was now facing Kym as she looked directly at Gray.

"I think Fred's only available after four today. That'll give you plenty of time to pick up Morgan and the kids," she said.

If he wasn't sitting in the middle of this very odd scenario, Gray might find it funny. It was obvious what Millie and Otis were trying to do. When in actuality, all Morgan had to do was call him and let him know she'd need a ride. He would have immediately told her he'd be there. He then realized she didn't have his phone number and he did not have hers, either. He'd had sex with this woman and had no way of communicating with her afterward. On any other day, when he was back in Miami, that might have been the ideal situation for Gray. Today, not so much.

"Tell your husband I'll be at his office at four," Gray told Millie. "After I pick up Morgan and the kids."

Kym huffed and then let out a little yelp as Otis traded places with Millie and now stood close enough that he could've lean over and sniffed Kym's hair.

Gray smiled then. This was definitely not a scenario that would have taken place back in Miami.

Morgan's first-grade classroom was located on the first floor of the old schoolhouse building. The structure had been renovated ten years ago, when there was an increase in enrollment—which came as a direct result of a blizzard six years prior that dropped three and a half feet of snow onto their tiny town. Prefab or modular structures, as some people called them, similar to the one Morgan lived in, had been situated in a *U* formation around the original building to add additional classroom space. The same had happened to the middle and high schools, which were originally two old mills that had been converted.

On Wednesdays, the last hour of her class time was normally quiet as her students were in the music room with Mrs. Ellersby. Earlier she'd found her holiday music playlist on her phone and was now playing it as she graded homework. The hope was that the music and the work would numb her mind to the nagging thoughts of Gray and last night—and having what was easily the best sex of her life on a couch, no less!

Her cheeks warmed and her stomach clenched each time the thought surfaced in her mind. How could she have been so careless? Lily had nightmares sometimes and Jack didn't always go to the bathroom before he got into bed. Either of them could have come out of their room and wandered into the living room, where they would have undoubtedly seen the light. Of course, they would have also seen something else. She cringed at the thought.

Gray was everything she'd thought he would be, taking into consideration that most of what she knew about him had come through secondhand stories from numerous people in town. The first time she'd seen him—well, actually, she'd bumped into him and felt every hard and tantalizing muscle of his chest—she'd known he would be a good lover. Not that she was all that experienced in the area. James hadn't been her first, but there had been only a couple before him. So, no, she would never consider herself to be a sex expert. Still, she could tell by the way he stood, with his legs partially spread and the strength in his arm as it had circled her waist. Morgan wasn't even going to add into the equation the moment she'd first felt his thick erection the night of the charity event. Yes, she'd been thinking about sleeping with him ever since that night. So what happened last night should not have come as any surprise.

Yet it did. She'd loved James with all her heart. How could she now so easily fall into bed—or wherever—with another man? Okay, she told herself with a heavy sigh,

James died three years ago. She had not been with any other man since then, had not even thought of dating, let alone sleeping with someone else. Until Gray. So logically, there was no reason why she shouldn't have jumped that fine-ass man's bones. None at all.

Then why did she feel like she'd made a colossal mistake?

"Hey there. You're much too pretty to be in such deep thought about anything," Harry said as he entered the room.

Morgan looked up from her desk to see his familiar face. He was wearing dark pants and a button-front shirt with the hardware store's logo on the front pocket. His boots made a dull sound as he crossed the tile floor, his face sporting the smile he almost always carried.

"Grading papers on who has the neatest coloring techniques is not as easy as you may think," she joked with him.

It was easy to joke with Harry because she'd known him forever. They talked as easily as brother and sister, but got along much better, she figured. Harry had taught her how to drive a stick shift. He'd given her and James a two-hundred-dollar gift voucher to his store. He'd also brought over the famous lasagna and tuna-mac casserole his mother made the day after James was buried. There wasn't a time in her life that Harry Reed had not been there and Morgan truly appreciated his friendship. But today, he was the last person she wanted to see.

"Well, you should stop grading those papers," he said as he came closer to the desk and looked down at her. "We can get the kids and head on over to the B and B, where my mom's cooked up her famous barbecue spare ribs, collard greens, and mac and cheese. Have dinner and then go out caroling. I know Lily's been looking forward to that. She couldn't stop talking about it the other day."

Yes, Lily loved to sing. The fact that Harry knew that made Morgan feel just a bit sadder. She was beginning to think that Wendy was right after all. Remembering the way that Harry had looked at Gray the other night when she'd picked up the kids had opened her eyes to something she felt guilty about not noticing before.

"That sounds wonderful," she told him. "But Granny's been making salads and sandwiches all day for the church. She has chicken salad and homemade bread. She called me earlier to tell me to stop by and get some leftovers."

Granny had made sandwiches for most of the celebrations in Temptation because everyone loved her chicken salad. The one time she'd tried to switch it up and brought tuna salad instead, there'd almost been a revolt.

Harry's smile didn't falter. "That sounds just as good. Nothing like Ms. Ida Mae's chicken salad on fresh white bread. I can take you over there and then we can head down to the town square. I had asked Otis about your car when he came into the store today and he said it wasn't ready yet."

"Ah, actually, I already have a ride," she told him.

Now Harry frowned. "I hope it's not with that Taylor guy. I heard you let him drive you in this morning. Look, you really need to be careful around him, Morgan. He's not who you think he is."

Morgan sat back in her chair then and simply looked up at Harry. This was the second time he'd warned her against Gray. The first time she'd brushed it off as him being another citizen who didn't want Gray interrupting their flow in Temptation. Now, she wasn't so sure that was all Harry was trying to say.

"Well, who is he then?" she asked out of curiosity. Maybe he knew something she didn't. Perhaps someone had told him something that was so ridiculously untrue that Morgan would have no choice but to set him straight.

Harry sighed, wiping a hand down his bald head. "I don't mean like that," he told her. "I'm just saying that he's not the type of person you're used to dealing with."

"Right. Because I have absolutely no experience dealing with grown men." She hadn't been offended when he'd said something similar the day before, but now she was. Did Harry really think she was some bubblehead who didn't know how to handle herself?

"Not that," he continued. "You do just fine around men. I mean, you know, you do just fine around town with all the people you've known forever. But nobody knows a thing about this guy. He left Temptation when he was just a kid and now he's back. Just like that. And we're all supposed to go around kissing his ass and making sure we suck up to him just so he won't sell some old run-down buildings. That's just bull!"

Now she was angry. How could Harry, of all people, act as if losing those buildings was no big deal to this town? One was actually the hospital, which they desperately needed since it was the only one in town.

"Well, I don't know about you, Harry, but I'd like to see those run-down buildings stay right here in this town. They're a part of our history and even if he's just returning to town, they're a part of Gray's history as well," she insisted.

"'Gray,' as you call him, doesn't give a crap about this town or those buildings. He's just worried about how much money they can make him," Harry quickly retorted.

Morgan wanted to yell. She wanted to tell him that Gray did care and that's why he was still here, giving her time to prove that the buildings should stay. But she couldn't because she really didn't know that what Harry just said wasn't true. Instead, she stood and shook her head.

"Somebody has to try and convince him to do otherwise. But since people in this town would rather sit back and talk a situation to death instead of getting up off their butts and doing something, I guess that someone has to be me," she said.

"He doesn't give a damn about you or anyone else in this town. The only use he has for a pretty woman is to get her in his bed."

Morgan's cheeks were on fire now. Her hands clenched at her sides as she tried valiantly to remain calm. Harry had no idea that she'd been with Gray in that way. He couldn't possibly know.

"I'm sorry," he said quickly. "I don't mean to upset you."

She was already shaking her head. "No. I'm not upset."

Morgan lied. She was upset and embarrassed and she wanted Harry to leave so that at least some of her emotions would subside.

"But I do have a ride home. Thank you so much for the offer, though. I guess I'll see you later at the caroling," she said when Harry made a motion to walk around the desk to where she was standing.

"Who's taking you home? I saw Wendy going to the hospital. She's working the night shift."

Okay, she hadn't secured a ride home, but Morgan would walk if she had to. It wasn't that far, even though she'd probably end up carrying Lily at some point. It didn't matter—she was not getting in Harry's truck.

"I am." Gray's deep voice sounded from the back of the classroom.

Harry turned and Morgan looked back to see Gray—dressed in another custom-fit and too-damn-sexy suit—walking toward them.

"She doesn't need to take rides from you in that fancy car," Harry said the moment Gray stood in front of him. "I can drive her around just fine."

That might be true, but Morgan didn't want him to. If she was still not completely convinced that Harry's feelings for her were much more than she wanted to reciprocate, she was positive now.

"That's okay, Harry. You don't have to spend your time worrying about me and my kids. Gray can drive us home," she said.

On one hand, she was still feeling too embarrassed and confused to be around Gray again. On the other, being with Harry was only going to feed his belief that there was something more between them. Morgan figured she was choosing the lesser of two evils.

He turned so fast and stared at her with such hurt and anger that Morgan almost faltered. Harry just continued to look at her as if waiting for her to say something different. She didn't and when he took a step toward her, Morgan saw Gray move. He was standing beside her in the next second.

"I'm ready whenever you are," Gray said, more to Harry than to her, she thought.

"I, um, just need to grab my things and go get the children. The bell should be ringing in a few minutes and the music class is near the back door," she said and moved to the side, away from both men.

"You don't get to come here and start barking orders," Harry told Gray.

Morgan looked up at him, still shocked that he was acting this way. "He's not giving anyone orders, Harry. He offered me a ride and I accepted. That's all."

"He's using you!" Harry shot back.

Morgan was angrier now than she'd thought she'd ever been before. "Using me? I'm a grown woman, Harry. And I'm pretty sure I'm capable of deciding who can give me a ride home. How that equates to him using me, I'm not sure."

"He's cozying up to you so that he can get you to give in about those damn buildings. That's what his type does to women. You don't see him coming to town to talk to any of the men about the buildings, do you? Hell, he should be dealing with Fred Randall, not you. You're just a teacher."

"That's enough," Gray said solemnly and once again moved closer to Morgan.

"Don't talk to me like that," Harry said, his voice booming in the room as he stepped closer to Gray.

"Stop it!" Morgan said, squeezing between the two men. "Harry, you're acting like an ass. I'm taking the ride home with Gray and since you think I'm nothing but a fluff-head female that can't tell when someone is using me or not, why don't you run along and find yourself someone else to insult!"

She didn't move and wouldn't look away when Harry stared down at her. It was a standoff, which she never would've imagined herself in, between two men who looked like they could probably do each other bodily harm. And her own adrenaline was drumming through her veins as if she might want to physically do some damage herself.

How dare Harry stand here and say all the crap he'd just said to her?

"You should leave," she heard Gray say from behind her.

"You," Harry said, pointing a finger at him. "Don't tell me what to do!"

"Go, Harry!" Morgan said. "I have a ride so there's no need for you to be here right now."

She felt a little like crap speaking to Harry—her long-time friend—that way, but hell, he deserved it after insulting her the way he just did.

Harry huffed and looked like he was going to actually take a punch at Gray, but he didn't. Instead, he stormed out of the classroom looking like a petulant child.

Chapter 9

Have a holly jolly Christmas! Have a holly jolly Christmas!

Gray rolled over, dropping an arm over his still-closed eyes, and grinned. Three days after they'd gone caroling, he could still hear Lily singing. She'd sung all that night, even as she ate chicken salad sandwiches and slurped chicken soup at the church. Every song they'd sung as they walked through the streets of Temptation, plus a few she'd added because she said she'd heard them on the radio earlier that day. Gray took that to mean two things—that she loved Christmas as much as her mother and that she also loved to sing.

Jack, on the other hand, wanted his sister to stop the minute she'd begun.

"She sings so loud," he'd complained as he walked beside Gray, holding his hand.

Lily, once again, was in Gray's arms. He never really knew how she ended up there, just that whenever he came near her, his arms seemed to itch to hold her. She was light as a feather, her cherublike cheeks soft as she nuzzled against him when she hugged him close. Was there ever anything that had felt this good? Gray had wondered as they'd moved through the streets.

"It's cold enough to snow," Jack had said after two or three songs.

He'd only sung the parts to the songs he knew, and usually only after Morgan had given him a questioning look because he was too quiet. Gray could totally relate. He wasn't a singer, either. Still, there were some lyrics he knew and when they came to a stop across from a row of homes where he was told the town's oldest living couple lived, they sang "O Come, All Ye Faithful" and Gray sang along. His mother had liked this song. She had sung it every holiday as they decorated their Christmas tree.

When he opened his eyes it was to a dim room and Gray immediately turned to look at the clock on the nightstand. It was after eight in the morning. He'd stayed up late last night going through the boxes of documents that Phil had sent from his father's house and his office. There'd been so many interesting things inside that Gray hadn't wanted to stop until he'd gone through each one.

One box had been full of Theodor's papers, copies of his divorce decree and all their birth certificates, which had been clipped together. Gray had frowned when he'd found those, then quickly put them to the side. His mother had the originals. Gray knew because he and Gemma had been the ones to go through Olivia's things after she'd died. Another box had large brown envelopes inside. On each envelope was one of the Taylor children's names. Gray shuffled through until he found the one with his name. He didn't realize how long he held that envelope in his hands until finally he decided to put that on the side, too.

There were also notes on what Theodor had planned

for the properties in Temptation. He'd wanted the hospital
to undergo another renovation, one that would include an
addition to the building. This would be called the Taylor
Generational Wing and would feature a state-of-the art
facility focusing specifically on infertility and the management and care of multiple pregnancies through multiple births. Theodor planned to put twenty-two million
dollars into the project.

Gray had been stunned.

The money from Theodor's estate had been equally di-
vided between him and his siblings. There was nothing
else. So where was Theodor getting this type of money
from?

Gray continued going through the other boxes, finding
pictures of them when they were young, many more than
he'd ever thought his father would have kept. There were
also bonds for each of them that probably should have been
kept in a safe-deposit box. Gray doubted they were worth
very much, but he'd put them on the table with the envelopes that he would have delivered to his siblings. The last
thing Gray had found before he'd headed to bed was a picture of his mother and father. It immediately reminded him
of the portrait he'd seen that day at the B and B, because
his mother was seated and his father stood behind her with
a hand on her shoulder. Theodor did not wear a hat, as the
man did in that portrait, but his facial expression was stoic,
almost to the point of being worried. His mother's expression was complacent, a look he'd seen her with much too
often. Still, his gaze had rested on his mother's wedding
ring and the gold band his father wore also. They were
committed to each other, regardless of what was going on
at that moment in time. Gray had wondered what had happened to that commitment.

Sleep had taken a while to come that night. He'd been
plagued by thoughts that he was more like his father than

he'd wanted to realize. The only thing that Gray had ever committed fully to was his company. He kept tabs on his siblings and communicated with them, because he knew his mother would have wanted them to stay together. But if there was something that needed to be done on the work front, he'd been known to put his family on the back burner. What did that say about the type of man he was?

With a sigh Gray climbed out of bed and went to the window. He looked out to see the farm blanketed in snow. The weatherman had predicted winter weather the night they'd gone caroling and Jack had been more than ready for it, but it never came. Now, days later, it looked like a world of white out there.

Gray went to take a quick shower. Once he was dressed he tried to bring some semblance of order to the papers and things from the boxes. He didn't want to repack them just yet because he was still taking notes on the buildings and Theodor's plans for them. He also wasn't ready to put away the envelopes with their names on them—something inside warned him that they were important. So important that looking at them right away was almost terrifying.

Gray made a call to Phil, instructing him to go back over all of his father's financials to see if he had some hidden stash of money that even Theodor's lawyers didn't know about.

"I want to know about every penny and every account with his name on it," Gray told his lawyer. Then he had a thought.

Turning with his cell phone in hand, Gray looked at the six brown envelopes still lying on the table where he'd put them last night.

"Check for bank accounts in our names," he told Phil. "Use each of the children's names and search the banks in and around the area of Temptation. Also, offshore accounts."

Phil probably had no idea what Gray was talking about—it was barely ten in the morning on a Saturday. Gray was positive that his thirty-year-old attorney, who liked to spend his nights in hot clubs and his days in the courtroom, was still rebounding from his Friday-night antics. Gray didn't care, he needed to find out if Theodor had been hiding money and why. His father had studied engineering while in college, only to return to Temptation, where he worked in the town council's office supervising and approving any road work and handing out permits for renovations to citizens. Once he'd left the town and his family, Theodor had opened the first Taylor Manufacturing Company in Syracuse, New York. There, the different engines he designed began being sold to various toy and clock companies.

Over the years Theodor made good money and then he'd been contracted by a Japanese auto company to build engines for their entire new lineup of cars and trucks. After that, Gray had watched the stock in Taylor Manufacturing soar and his father become a billionaire before he turned fifty. To an extent, Gray knew that was part of what drove him. He'd always wanted to be better than Theodor Taylor.

When the call was finished, Gray grabbed his coat and a change of clothes. What he had planned for the day was bound to get messy, he thought with a smile as he left his room and ventured out into the blustery cold morning.

His car was not made to be driven in a foot of snow, but with the help of Jim Coolridge, who was already up and out shoveling his walkway so that he could get out and tend to his animals, Gray's car was finally on the road. He drove slowly, as there'd been no plow coming down these streets. He marveled at the fluffy white substance that hung on trees and covered the landscape because it had been so long since he'd last seen it. When the weatherman had called for snow and Gray knew he'd still be in town, he'd ordered some things online. Luckily, they'd arrived yesterday morning. He wiggled his toes in the insulated boots he was now wearing. They were oddly comfortable, even if the puffy ski jacket he wore was beginning to make him sweat in the heated interior of the car.

When he pulled up in front of Morgan's house, Gray couldn't wait to go inside. He felt like a kid again as he slumped through the snow, only to frown as he saw that the snow had once again started to fall and that Morgan's sidewalk was covered with it.

"Got a shovel?" he asked the moment she answered the door.

"What?" she asked with a confused expression, obviously not used to men showing up at her door on Saturday mornings.

"So I can shovel the sidewalk," he told her.

While she was standing there looking perplexed, Gray smiled. He liked seeing her hair matted to one side and her thick purple robe belted tightly around her slim waist. He knew that as cold as it was out there, the last thing he should be thinking about was how sexy she looked, but he couldn't help it. He wanted to grab her up in his arms and swing her around. He'd nuzzle her neck the same way Lily did his and enjoy the softness of her.

"Yay! Mr. Gray's here! We're gonna make snowmen!" Jack yelled from where he now stood behind his mother.

"Can we, Mama? Can we go out and make snowmen now?" Jack asked.

"It's cold and it's still snowing and—" Morgan stammered.

"I know I'm from Miami, but I'm thinking these are the best conditions to make snowmen," Gray told her.

"Uh-huh. Uh-huh. It is. Best conditions, Mama. The best!" Jack continued, this time pulling on the belt of Morgan's robe.

"Mr. Gray's here in the snow! He's not wearing a suit, Mama," Lily noted when she peeked her head around Morgan's other side.

Gray shrugged. "You might as well toss me the shovel and get them dressed. They're never going to give you any peace if you don't."

Her frown said she'd deal with him later. The children's excited laughter as she backed away and closed the door meant she was going to take his suggestion. The shovel was tossed outside moments later, followed by the door slamming.

Two hours later it was still snowing. Morgan had never seen such huge flakes as they fell all around them. She'd bundled up the kids and dressed herself warmly and had come outside to see Gray moving the snow with ease. He'd been almost finished shoveling the walkway at that point and she'd gone over to help him, while Jack and Lily had instantly fallen onto the ground to make snow angels.

"You make one, Mama," Lily insisted, coming over to grab Morgan's hand.

"Let me finish this first," Morgan said.

Lily pouted and seconds later, Morgan felt herself being lifted from the spot where she stood. With a yelp she wrapped her arms around Gray's neck as he'd easily scooped her up into his arms. "You wouldn't," she warned just seconds before he'd grinned down at her and then dropped her into the snow.

Stunned, embarrassed, irritated. None of those words meant a thing in comparison to Lily's and Jack's immediate giggles. They both jumped happily on her as she lay there and Morgan hugged them close. She loved when they were happy. That was the reason she'd hustled them to the side, got up and then fell back in the snow on her own, spreading her legs and arms to make an angel.

Gray was standing beside her when she got up.

"Beautiful," he said, and used his gloved hands to wipe flecks of snow from her face.

"I've always been good at making snow angels," she told him.

He shook his head and whispered, "Not the angel."

Jack's snowman took priority after that and the four of them worked long and hard to build the biggest and friendliest one they could. Morgan tracked snow through the house to find a scarf, an old thick Magic Marker for its nose and spare buttons for the eyes.

"He doesn't look like Frosty," Lily proclaimed as they stood back and admired their handiwork.

"That's because his name is George," Gray said. "George the snowman."

"That sounds silly," Jack proclaimed and then laughed. "That's our snowman, George. Take a picture so we can send it to Aunt Wendy and Granny!"

Gray dug his phone out of his coat pocket and snapped a picture of George.

"All of you go stand beside him," Gray instructed and they followed.

Morgan stood beside George while Jack and Lily kneeled down in front of him. When the kids scrambled out of the way, tossing more snow at each other, Morgan thought she saw another flash. She looked around and then back at Gray, who snapped another picture of her.

"What are you doing?"

"Making a memory," he replied instantly.

Later that afternoon, once Morgan had gotten the kids and herself out of their wet clothing and fixed grilled cheese sandwiches and tomato soup for everyone, she and Gray sat in the living room alone.

"They'll sleep for a couple hours they're so worn out," she told him.

He'd taken off his wet clothes and slipped on a pair of sweatpants that should have definitely been banned for any man built like Gray to wear. His T-shirt was fitted, his feet covered in white socks as he sat on her couch, looking as if he belonged there. With a resigned sigh to not entertain any more guilty thoughts about James, she'd taken a seat on the other end of the couch. The only other furniture in her living room besides the couch was an old recliner, which had a tendency to recline on its own. She usually steered clear of it while the kids loved to play on it. Which was probably the reason it was broken.

"They had fun," Gray said. He was holding a mug of hot chocolate she'd just made for the two of them. His big hands wrapped tightly around the Scooby-Doo mug. "I'd forgotten how much fun it could be to play in the snow."

"I'll bet you and your siblings had a great time in that big yard. The property surrounding that house is so spacious and totally conducive to a big family," she said before hurrying to sip from her cup in fear she had said too much.

Gray sat with his elbows on his knees and stared down into his cup.

"We played all day in the summer. After breakfast we'd head right outside. Me, Garrek and Gage, we liked to build forts and keep the girls out." He chuckled. "Gemma and Gia were always plotting ways to get inside. But Gen, that's what we call Genevieve, she didn't care. She was always the more serious one out of all of us. She learned how to read first and never let any of us forget that she could do it best."

"Wendy did most everything better than me. She ran faster, did better splits and cartwheels. She even sounded better yelling cheers than I did," Morgan said and then shrugged. "But I had kids first and she hates that."

"My mother always said she was glad she decided to keep all her babies. She'd wanted a big family and she'd gotten it in a one-shot deal," he said.

Morgan couldn't help but feel admiration for Olivia Taylor. Having twins had been quite a task for her, so there was no way she could imagine giving birth to sextuplets.

"I imagine it was hard for her, the pregnancy and everything."

"The press was the hardest part," Gray said. "She never liked them being around all the time. I guess that's why I don't, either."

Morgan sighed. "Granny said they've been driving all around town talking to people and speculating about what you're going to do."

He shook his head. "It shouldn't matter to them. I mean, it's just a story they get to tell. Just like they told the story about my family before, only they got that one all wrong."

"No," Morgan admitted. "It probably doesn't really matter to them. But it does to me. Especially because after I lost James, this town and the people here were all I had left. They took me and my kids in and they showered us with their love and generosity. It's my home and it just matters," she told him with a quiet shrug.

Gray sat back on the couch then and looked over at her. She didn't turn away, although his gaze was intense. It was also needy and Morgan couldn't bear not to be there for him. She suspected that nobody had been there for Gray all these years. He was a fixer and so he fixed things, but he didn't share and he didn't grieve. She thought that was very sad.

"I know it matters to you," he told her. "I'm trying to do the right thing here, Morgan. I just need to figure out what that is."

She nodded. "I understand."

She did and then she didn't. What she thought was so

simple, she imagined was much harder for someone with the feelings Gray was harboring.

"My father had plans for those buildings. I want to know exactly what those plans were and how he was going to implement them."

"And then what? Will you carry out his plans even though you still hold so much resentment toward him?"

He frowned and then took a sip from his cup. "I'm going to do what I think is best for everyone involved. I'll ask my siblings when I make a decision and then I'll go from there."

"The community center has been the hub for our theater program. Kids in the town over have taken school trips out here to see plays. It doesn't bring in a lot of money, but I was thinking that we could invite other theater groups here, larger ones to put on plays maybe around the holidays. We have lots of great shops here so tourists could not only pay to see really great professional plays, but also shop around and purchase unique gifts," she offered.

"And what about the hospital?" he asked.

Morgan leaned forward to set her mug on the coffee table. Then she turned, lifting one leg to rest on the couch as she faced Gray. "Well, for starters, it's the only full-service medical facility we have. Doc Silbey still has his clinic down on River Street, but he's getting older and mostly only tends to minor bumps and bruises. Besides, my sister works at the hospital and so do a lot of other people. Where will they find work? What will happen when Granny finally cracks someone over the head with that cane of hers because they ticked her off?"

He laughed at that. Morgan liked his laugh, the deep rumble that came bursting out of his chest. She was liking way too much about this man.

"I can actually see that happening," he told her when he'd regained a bit of his composure.

"Me, too," she said, and had to chuckle herself because he'd started laughing again.

Then she sobered a bit, propped her arm on the back of the couch and leaned her head on her hand. "What I'm saying is that we have a use for the buildings here. Sure, they may need to be renovated, but they also need to stay. If you sell them to someone, who knows what they'll want to do with them. They might even think it's best to just tear them down. So I hope you'll consider all this when you make your final decision."

"I will," he said. "I'm going to consider something else, too."

"What's that?" she asked casually. Throughout the day she'd grown more and more comfortable with Gray being there. Though that wasn't totally true, she admitted to herself. The comfort had been growing in the last week as he'd picked her up for work and brought her home after work, as if it was their daily routine. When he showed up the second morning, Morgan decided not to argue the transportation issue anymore. The kids loved riding in the fancy car with the heated seats and Morgan kind of liked not having to hear Wendy complain about getting up too early in the morning to come and get her while her car was still in the shop.

"How much I like kissing you," he answered.

No matter how comfortable she thought she felt, his words still caught her off guard.

She cleared her throat. "I'm, ah, I'm not sure we should go down this road again."

Gray moved closer to her. "I'm not sure we can avoid it."

He was right and Morgan couldn't figure out anything to say to rebut his statement. That was all Gray needed to react. If she gave him the smallest opening, he'd fill it, quickly and completely. His hand cupped her face in a motion so soft and endearing she sighed.

"I never imagined a man like you coming into my life," she admitted. "And I'm sure I'm not the type of woman you usually spend your time with."

His thumb rubbed along her cheek as a smile slowly spread across his face. "That just means that neither of us were thinking enough of ourselves."

"Gray," she sighed again, her eyes fluttering as she saw him moving closer.

"Yes?" he answered, his lips just a whisper away from hers.

"I like kissing you, too."

Chapter 10

He wanted to see all of her this time and he didn't want her on a damn couch. So Gray took Morgan by the hand and they both stood. She stepped close to him and wrapped her free arm around his waist.

"This won't end well," she said softly, resting her forehead against his chest.

He leaned forward and kissed the top of her head. "I don't want to talk about the end," he told her. "I don't want to talk at all."

In the next instant he was lifting her into his arms, cradling her small frame against his chest as he walked back toward her bedroom. She lay her head on his shoulder and Gray looked down at her as he stepped into her room. Using his foot, he closed the door behind them and moved closer to her bed. The room was small. She'd taken the smaller one and had given her children the larger room. Her queen-size bed barely fit, leaving room for only one nightstand on that side of the room. There was a window and right next to the door was her dresser.

Standing at the foot of her bed, Gray let her down slowly, loving the way her body felt moving along his. She kept her palms flat on his chest and looked up at him. Gray leaned down, taking her lips in a soft and slow kiss that only stoked the fire already brimming inside him.

What was it about this woman? She was absolutely right when she had said she was not the type of woman he dated. He could count on one hand how many female bedrooms he'd seen over the years, preferring a hotel room to the personal space of him or the woman he was with. Had he ever known any of their family members? No. He was certain of that fact.

Gray knew that Morgan liked lots of sugar and a little cream in her coffee and that she drank that coffee from a Tinker Bell mug every morning. He knew that her shoe size was an eight and a half—he'd learned that when he'd helped the kids pull her boots off earlier when they'd come inside. She laughed a lot when her children were around. Her eyes danced with the action and her cheeks lifted high on her face.

When her arms came up to wrap around his neck, Gray wrapped his tighter around her petite body. He now held her so close to him that he felt the moment she came up on tiptoe to meet his demands. Pulling away from the kiss, he set her slowly on the bed. She'd changed into thin pants that left absolutely nothing to the imagination. Her full bottom had enticed him terribly as she'd moved throughout the kitchen fixing their lunch. Now, he pulled those pants down her legs slowly. They trembled slightly and he touched one thigh, while dropping a soft kiss on the other.

He removed her shirt, his fingers brushing against the pale green lace of her bra. When he'd tossed the shirt to the side, Gray couldn't help himself—he leaned in, dragging his tongue over the hill of cleavage. She sucked in a breath and he moved to the other breast to lick the smooth skin there as well. When her hand went to the back of his head, his erection throbbed, pressing against the restraint of his boxers and his sweatpants.

Her hands were fast and before he could take another breath, Morgan was reaching down the fabric of his pants, grasping his length in her palm. The breath didn't come and he almost choked, pleasure spiking through his blood. Gray hurriedly unsnapped her bra so he could get his mouth on her pert nipples. Morgan moved just as quickly, as she pushed at his pants and boxers, until she could wrap her bare hands around his length, stroking him from the base to the tip. Gray moaned, closing his eyes and suckling her breast with more urgency than ever. He thrust his hips into her strokes, loving the warmth and the desire that continued to spread like wildfire at her touch.

"Off!" she moaned and tried to push at his pants once more.

With Herculean strength he pulled away from her, her breast leaving his mouth with a popping sound. Gray pulled at his clothes, tossing them wherever they fell in her room. He'd clean up later, he told himself. All that mattered now was her.

She slid back farther on the bed until her head rested on the pillows. Then she let her legs open wide, her arms lifting to him. Had he ever seen anything as beautiful as Morgan lying naked on a bright rainbow-colored bedspread? Gray didn't think so. He did think, however, that he was going to make a fool of himself and come right then at the sight of her tender folds open and damp with her arousal for him.

"You were right," he said, his voice gruff as he climbed on the bed, moving slowly toward her. "You're not like any other woman I've ever met."

When he thought he saw her tense, Gray touched the inside of her thighs, pushing them farther apart until he leaned forward and dragged his tongue through her moist center. "You're so much more," he whispered before touching his tongue to her soft, wet flesh once more.

She gasped and then moaned as he continued, lifting her hips as if she wanted to feed him. That was just fine with Gray because he was hungry, so damn hungry for her. She was delicious, soft, hot, sweet. He couldn't get enough as he delved deeper, his fingers clenching her thighs. He was intoxicated—that's the only way Gray could think to describe the woozy feeling he had each time he inhaled the scent of desire and tasted her thick nectar. The more she moved against his mouth, the hungrier he became. He didn't think he would ever get his fill of her.

"Gray!" she moaned and he knew she was trying her best to be quiet.

He wanted to help her with that, but he couldn't stop. Each time he told himself that he'd had enough and tried to pull back, he opened his eyes and look down at her plump flesh so moist and delectable, and all for him. Yes, he told himself, she was for him. All of her.

When her body trembled beneath him and she clenched the back of his head until the waves of pleasure had finally abated, Gray moved over her. He slipped inside of her in one thrust, filling her completely and loving every inch of his length she'd sucked into her waiting abyss.

It was heaven. No, for Gray this was so much more. It was a place he'd never imagined, a feeling he'd never conceived. Buried to the hilt inside of Morgan, he closed his eyes to the onslaught of feelings. On the one hand he wanted to hold her tightly to him. On the other, he wanted her in every position he could visualize, taking every bit of this desire he had for her. He wanted her release, again and again. He wanted her moans against his mouth, her softness against his skin. If he could hear her voice…

"Gray," she moaned when he thrust deep into her once more, as if on cue.

"Say it again," he told her. "Please say it again."

Because if she did he'd know without a doubt this was where he belonged. This place, right here, right now, was made just for him.

"Yes, Gray," she whispered. "Yes!"

"Yes," he said, echoing her. "Yes!"

This was where he was supposed to be. He moved in and out of her, dropping kisses over her forehead, down her nose and onto her waiting lips. She wrapped her arms around his shoulders, her legs around his waist and held on tight. He stopped thinking—hell, he may have even stopped breathing, she felt so good.

When she pushed against him and he rolled over onto his back, Gray thought he'd never seen anything so beautiful. He'd been wrong. She looked like a sex goddess rising over him with her hair slightly mussed, her high pert breasts staring down at him. When she opened her legs and straddled him, Gray moaned. He grabbed her hips, guiding her. She didn't need the help, he thought as she grabbed his erection with ease, positioning him so that she could lower herself onto his shaft. It was hot and exciting, the connection striking him like ten thousand bolts of lightning.

She lowered herself slowly and Gray watched with intense pleasure as his length disappeared inside of her. When she was completely impaled he squeezed her hips, reached his hands up to cup her breasts and whispered her name this time.

"Morgan," he said. "My sweet and hot Morgan."

She rode him then, letting her head fall back as she arched over him, driving him crazy with desire. When they finally laced their fingers together, holding their arms above them, Gray pumped wild and fast inside her, loving the sight of her keeping up with his pace, her breasts moving and her mouth open as she moaned her pleasure. They came together this time, squeezing each other's fingers and trying like hell not to yell out as the intense feelings of desire completely washed over them.

Dinner was homemade pizzas.

The reason why there was now red sauce splashed over the counters and on the table. The mozzarella-and-Romano-cheese mix was sprinkled across the floor in almost a direct path from where Lily and Jack had carried their handfuls from the counter to the table, where their individual pizzas were being prepared. It had only taken two trips for Morgan to realize it was smarter to move the bowl of cheese to the table with the rest of the ingredients. The table was small so she'd been trying to leave plenty of room for the two of them to work, but that had only created more of an issue as they bumped into each other as they moved back and forth.

As for Gray, well, his white T-shirt had red splashes all over it. Then while Jack was trying to carry the tray with his pizza to the oven, he'd even dropped a huge glob of pepperoni soaked in sauce and cheese on Gray's foot. To say it had been an adventure in the kitchen was definitely an understatement.

While the pizzas cooked, Gray had volunteered to take the twins into the living room to watch *Frosty the Snowman*. After about two minutes of feeling grateful, Morgan realized he'd done it to get out of cleaning the kitchen. She smiled and shook her head as she went to the side of the refrigerator to retrieve the broom.

Her cell phone, which had been charging all day on the counter by the blender, rang just as she began sweeping.

"Hey," she said after seeing Wendy's name on the caller ID.

"Hi," Wendy replied. "How are you guys holding up in this storm? Need me to come over with anything?"

"No, we're good. How are you and Granny fairing?" Morgan asked.

They were probably at each other's throats, which was their norm. Two years ago the doctor had told Granny she needed that cane and glasses. She hated both. Wendy and Morgan had decided that their grandmother probably needed more in the way of daily care, so since Wendy was still single and had no kids, she'd given up her apartment and moved in with Ida Mae. They'd been battling ever since.

"She's in the kitchen cooking. You know that's the only thing that keeps her quiet. That and *Jeopardy*," Wendy added with a chuckle. "What are you guys doing? Been out in the snow yet? I know Jack's been worrying you to death about it," Wendy continued.

Morgan moved around the kitchen sweeping up everything that had fallen onto the floor, which was a lot. "We went out this morning when Gray came over."

The moment she said the words, Morgan knew they were a mistake.

"Gray came over in a snowstorm?" Wendy asked with more than a little suspicion laced in her tone. "Wait, is he still there?"

Morgan couldn't lie, not to her sister.

"Yes, he is," she said simply and prayed that would be the end of it.

No such luck.

"And just what is he doing now? Or maybe I should ask what are you doing? That might be the better question," Wendy said. Morgan could hear the grin in Wendy's voice. "Is my little sister having a sordid affair with the new guy in town?"

Morgan really hated how that sounded, but she couldn't deny it. She was, and actually, she was really liking it.

"Okay, I am," she told Wendy. "But it's not as sordid and scandalous as the way you make it sound."

"Oh, really? Then tell me what it is. Because from where I'm sitting, you had sex with him just a few days after you met him and if you haven't already, I bet you'll have sex with him again tonight."

"What makes you say that?" Morgan asked, unable to really sound surprised by Wendy's statement, considering she and Gray had not too long ago done exactly what her sister was suggesting.

"Hello, we're in the middle of a snowstorm. What do people do in snowstorms besides shovel snow? Make love," Wendy quipped. "You remember how the school became overcrowded in the first place. In another five years we'll be building another extension to those buildings."

"Stop it," Morgan insisted. "It's not like that."

"Mmm-hmm," Wendy said and began to laugh.

"I'm hanging up now," Morgan told her.

"Okay, okay, look, I know my sister so I think I know that you're serious when you say it's not some scandalous affair. So what is it? Are you two falling in love or something? Oh, that would be awesome. I saw him coming out of the school the other day with the twins and he's great with them. Wouldn't it be wonderful if you did fall in love and get married? The twins would have a father and you'd have someone to share your life with. Plus he's rich so you'd definitely get to move out of Temptation into some big ol' house with fabulous furniture and jewelry."

Wendy loved jewelry and shoes. She also enjoyed dying her hair different colors and eating coconuts and fancy chocolates.

Morgan sighed.

"No, definitely not all that. And I don't care about

Gray's money. I'm—I'm just enjoying this for right now. That's all. Can't I do that?" she asked.

"You definitely can," her sister replied. "You deserve to enjoy whatever moments you can find. You were a widow at a young age, a mother, too—of course you deserve some happiness. I'm just jealous, that's all. Gray's hot and loaded." Wendy laughed.

Morgan shook her head, but couldn't help but smile. "Yeah. He is."

He was also spending the night with her, which Morgan realized hours later, after dinner and the many holiday movies they watched.

Last night had been the most fun Gray had at Christmastime since he was a young boy. That giddy feeling in the pit of his stomach that started around the first of December when he was a kid had made a home there now. He'd already planned to go into the coffee shop at his earliest convenience so he could go online and buy all the things Jack and Lily had told him they were expecting Santa to bring.

Sometime in the middle of the night, he'd realized he wanted to see their faces when they opened their gifts. He wanted to hear their laughter and experience their joy. He wanted a family.

Several hours had passed after this morning's pancake-and-scrambled-egg breakfast that Gray had tried to help Morgan prepare. He was a horrible cook, but he'd figured cracking eggs wouldn't be too difficult. He was so wrong and thus they'd had a few crunchy moments when eating their eggs.

Gray had been in the living room playing a board game that the twins were definitely winning when he realized Morgan had been gone for quite a bit of time. She'd excused herself when her phone rang. It had taken a few minutes, about ten he recalled, as he looked at his watch again and moved toward the bedroom, where he suspected Morgan had gone. He told himself he wasn't the jealous type. He'd never had a reason to be. Yet, something had nagged at him about her being gone on a call for this long. Something he wasn't too keen on acknowledging.

"Everything all right?" he asked when he saw her staring out the window in her bedroom.

She jumped at the sound of his voice.

"Ah, yeah. Everything's fine. I'll be out in a minute," she told him.

That was meant to dismiss him, but Gray didn't leave the room.

"Who were you talking to?" he asked her.

The look she gave him was nothing short of pissed off. "I don't think that's any of your business, Gray. I mean, we haven't known each other long enough for you to question me."

Gray knew then that whomever she'd spoken to on the phone had upset her and he was lucky enough to be the one standing in the room with her at the moment. He was the one that was undoubtedly going to take the brunt of her anger.

He crossed the room, coming to stop right in front of her. Yet Gray was careful to remain far enough away. If she wanted to take a swing, she'd miss, but he was close enough if she needed a shoulder to lean on instead.

"I'm not questioning you," he told her. "I'm concerned."

"Concerned about what? Your precious buildings?" she snapped and then shook her head. "I'm sorry. That's not fair."

"What's going on, Morgan? Who upset you?"

She clenched the phone in her hand, then brought it up to her forehead, tapping it there while she waited. "I should have known better," she began. "I've lived here all my life so I should know how they are by now."

"You should know how who is?" Gray asked, getting a sinking suspicion he wasn't going to like where their conversation was going.

Sighing heavily, Morgan tossed the phone onto her bed and looked at him. "That was my grandmother on the phone. She was calling to tell me that it doesn't look good for a single mother to have a man spending the night at her house."

Gray could only stare at her in disbelief, even though he was familiar with the rumor mill in Temptation.

"Somebody apparently rode by and saw your car here. They couldn't wait to get on the phone to start spreading it around. Granny said that Martina from the church just called her to ask what was going on between us," Morgan told him.

"Wow." It was all Gray could say at first. "I've heard the saying 'word travels fast' but I never knew that meant it traveled through a snowstorm," he told her. "Who the hell was out last night or yesterday in the storm to know that I was here? And why were they driving down this road again today to see if I was still here?"

"My first guess is Otis," she said. "He has a plow that he hitches to the front of his truck and uses to clean the main streets. The town council hires a professional but sometimes they take a while to get here."

"So Otis ran back and told who? Because I don't see him picking up the phone and passing along this news," Gray said, like it even mattered.

"He probably would have stayed at the B and B to help out Mr. Reed with the guests and getting their vehicles shoveled out," Morgan said and then she paused.

"What?" Gray asked.

"Your assistant is staying at the B and B," she told him.

"Kym? She wouldn't call anyone in this town to tell them a damn thing. She barely likes speaking to the people around here." That was certainly true, as was the fact that Kym was still in town. Each day that Gray had spoken to her she'd had another reason to stay. He'd decided that he had other things to focus on besides Kym. He wondered briefly if that had been a mistake.

"Yeah, I heard that about her," Morgan added. "But if Otis mentioned your name and Kym was around, I'm sure her diamond-stud ear would have perked right up."

She was probably right about that, Gray thought.

"What about Harry?"

"What about him?" she asked.

"Would he call around and tell people?"

She seemed to think about it for a moment. At the same time Gray heard something outside. He looked out the window to see a local news truck pulling up and cursed.

"I guess it doesn't matter who called who, the reporters know now so the whole world is about to find out," he said.

Morgan came up behind him, a hand going quickly over her mouth. "Why would they care?" she asked.

"Because I'm a Taylor and I'm back in Temptation. It's news for them. We've always been just news to them."

They stood there for a few moments in silence, watching as the cameramen set up just a few feet away from Morgan's house. The snow had stopped sometime in the middle of the night and now the sun was shining brightly. Gray had gone out again last night to shovel the walkway. If he'd known it would have just make things easier for the reporters to get closer to the house, he wouldn't have. But there was nothing he could do about it now.

"Let's give them something to report," Morgan said from beside him.

"What?" he asked.

She looked up to him. "If they're here it's because

somebody already told them that this is where you were. They obviously want something to report, so let's give it to them."

Gray couldn't believe she was saying that. "What did you have in mind?"

Chapter 11

It had been over two weeks since Gray, Morgan and the twins made national headlines as they'd decorated Morgan's Christmas tree in front of an open window and an entire news crew.

Now, just five days before Christmas, Morgan was at the community center practicing the play with her kids again. The town was abuzz with festivities. All up and down Main Street, holiday music played through the speakers that had been hung outside the buildings. Storefronts were decorated with everything from Santa and his reindeer, to snow villages and huge decorative gift boxes. It looked like a scene out of an old movie and Morgan loved walking through the street to get to the community center.

She'd told Gray that she had a ride because Wendy was off work that night and could help her with the rehearsal. He'd seemed a little distant when she'd spoken to him, but Morgan had forced herself not to think about it. Wendy was meeting her at the community center, so she and the kids had walked from the school. It was a chilly day, but Jack and Lily loved playing in the new snow that had fallen just yesterday.

"Granny says with all the snow we've had so far, we probably won't get any now on Christmas Day. It would have been nice to have a white Christmas," Lily stated as Morgan worked on the last of the props for the play.

"She might be right," Morgan replied, looking up quickly at Lily.

Her daughter had been laughing so much lately that the return of her usual solemn tone caused Morgan to worry.

"We haven't had a white Christmas in Temptation since I was a little baby," Morgan told her. "But it'll still be Christmas."

Lily pouted. "Will it still be Christmas if Mr. Gray leaves?"

Morgan didn't know how to answer that question. In the past few weeks, Gray had been with them almost every day. If he wasn't driving them somewhere, he was stopping by her house. He played with the kids while Morgan caught up on housework or worked on lesson plans. Last night, he'd even taken them to Sal's Italian Bistro for dinner. Jack had so many cannoli he'd had a stomach ache by the time they had arrived home.

"Christmas always comes, regardless of who's here or who's not," Morgan finally answered.

"Like it came all those times while Daddy was gone," Lily added for clarification.

The words tugged at Morgan's heart.

"Yes, baby, just like that," she answered.

Lily shook her head. "But Mr. Gray's not dead. He can be here for Christmas, can't he, Mama?"

Morgan sighed. She was in big trouble now. Her mind had warned against getting involved with Gray from the very start. She'd known that he had no plans of staying in Temptation, and yet she hadn't cared. Everything that had happened between Morgan and Gray had been for her pleasure only. How her children would bond with him and how they were going to feel in turn when he left town had not been a big enough priority for her. Dammit.

"Of course he's staying for Christmas," Jack said when he came over to join them. "You heard him say we were gonna put that train set that Santa's going to bring me together. I'm gonna be the conductor and Mr. Gray's gonna work for me."

Her son spoke so proudly. He was poking out his chest and looking as serious as an adult as he talked to his sister.

"There's no need to worry. We're gonna have the best Christmas ever!" Jack continued.

Morgan didn't know if that was true or not, just as she didn't know if Ethan was going to recite the lines they'd rehearsed for the past few weeks, or make up his own on Christmas Eve. What she did know, and probably the only thing Morgan thought she could control, was that she needed to draw a line between her, Gray and her kids before it was really too late.

A few minutes before rehearsal was over, Morgan jumped at a tap on her shoulder. This was the fifth time they'd gone over the Jacob Marley scene. Even though she knew the ghost was really Cabe Dabney's voice and Lily and Wendy rattling the chains, Morgan was starting to feel a little edgy.

"Sorry," Harry said. "Didn't mean to frighten you."

"Oh, no," Morgan told him, shaking her head. "I'm fine. How are you, Harry?"

She hadn't seen much of him in the past couple of weeks, not since the blowup they'd had in her classroom that day.

"I'm good. How've you been?" he asked, thrusting his hands in the pockets of his work pants.

Morgan tried to smile, but she was really tired and had a headache. A big part of her wished the twenty-fourth would hurry up and get here so she could be finished with this play. Wendy, of course, had thought what she said was hilarious when Morgan had said it out loud about half an hour ago.

"I'm hanging in there," she admitted with a sigh. "The kids are really excited, though. It's going to be a nice production." Lord, she hoped so, she thought as she closed her eyes.

"That's good. You know my mom's spearheading the potluck that's going to be held in the kitchen here that night," he told her.

Morgan nodded. "Yes, I heard. That's so generous of her. Granny said she's not making chicken salad again. She's baking cakes instead. I think she said a Kentucky butter cake, a rum cake and a pineapple upside-down cake."

Harry pulled a hand out of his pocket to rub over his stomach. "Then I'm definitely coming to see the play."

Morgan chuckled and for a moment it felt like old times between them. The easy rapport they'd always had was back and she was glad. She really hadn't wanted any hard feelings over what had happened between them.

"I can't wait until it gets here," she said. "Is that why you stopped by, to drop off some things for your mother?"

"Oh, no. Smitty finished with your car so I told him I'd drive it over," Harry told her.

"That's fantastic! You don't know what it's like to be at someone else's beck and call until your car breaks down. Thanks so much, Harry," she said and on impulse gave him a hug.

Harry hugged her back. Tightly.

"What's the special occasion?" Wendy asked when she walked up to where Morgan and Harry stood. Morgan pushed away from Harry to turn to her sister.

"Harry brought my car over. It's fixed," she told Wendy. "Now you don't have to drive me home."

Wendy was looking at Harry, one hand on her hip. "Oh, did he now? That sure was nice of you, Harry."

"No big deal. I just wanted to make sure she got it as quickly as possible," he said.

"Uh-huh," Wendy commented and nodded.

Morgan's cell phone vibrated in her back pocket and she pulled it free to read the text message. It was from Gray. He wanted to know if she needed a ride home. She hurriedly typed that she wouldn't because her car was now fixed. He replied instantly, saying that was great, and then asked if she would mind coming by the resort. There was something he wanted to tell her.

"She can just drop me off at the B and B once she leaves here," Harry was saying when Morgan looked up to see that he and Wendy were still standing there.

"Ah, actually," Morgan said, "I was going to ask Wendy to take the kids home with her. Granny wants them to help her wrap presents."

"Sure," Wendy said with a slow nod toward Harry. "And since your parents' B and B is right around the corner, I can drop you off, too."

Harry immediately looked to Morgan.

"That's great," Morgan said. "I have to just get the kids together so they'll be ready when their parents show up. Thanks again, Harry."

Morgan replied to Gray's text as she walked away. Tomorrow she'd have to buy Wendy some of those chocolate-covered raisins she loved so much from Mr. Edison's candy shop. Not only was her sister taking her kids, but she'd also thwarted Harry's plan to be alone with Morgan.

* * *

It had been a while since Morgan had been out to the Coolridge farm. Two years ago, with revenue from the farm tight, the Coolridges decided to use the space where the family used to breed horses to hopefully make ends meet. As far as Morgan knew, they were still barely scraping by as there didn't seem to be that many tourists who wanted to come stay on a farm without the basic amenities of the real world.

She walked up the steps to the Owner's Suite, where Netta had informed her Gray was staying. For a moment Morgan had thought about texting Gray and asking where his room at the farm was instead of alerting someone else to her presence there. Then she decided *what the hell*. The entire town already knew she and Gray were involved ever since she'd had the brilliant idea for them to decorate her Christmas tree in front of the news cameras.

"Hi," she said when he opened the door.

"Hey. Come on in," Gray said before walking away.

The first thing Morgan realized as she stepped inside and took off her coat was that she'd never seen Gray like this before. He was disheveled. He wore jeans, which she'd gotten used to over the past couple of weeks. There was no doubt that this man could wear the hell out of a suit, but the jeans gave him an even more dangerous and rugged look that she found enticing as well. Closing the door behind her, Morgan also noted that he wasn't wearing any shoes and his T-shirt, which he would normally have neatly tucked into his pants, was out and wrinkled.

There were boxes and papers all over the place. A tablet sat on the table amidst more papers and files. On the bed were his cell phone and briefcase. Something was definitely going on with him and despite her resolve to draw the line between them, Morgan wanted to know what it was. She wanted to help, if she could.

"What's going on, Gray?" she asked.

"I found it," he said.

He ran a hand down the back of his head and sighed heavily. "I found it," Gray repeated.

"You found what?" she asked. It looked like he could easily *lose* something in this room.

"The money," he told her, a slow grin creeping onto his face.

"What money?"

Gray was a multimillionaire, Morgan knew that. So watching him look excited and relieved over money left her baffled.

"My father's money. I mean, the money he put aside for the town," Gray continued.

He moved quickly to the table, picked up a folder and thrust it toward Morgan as he continued to talk.

"It was Fred," he began. "He's the one that told Millie about my dad's plans for the hospital. Remember you told me about that?"

Morgan looked up from the bank statements she was reading and nodded. "Yes, I remember."

"Well, I found the plans. They're right here," Gray said, picking up another file. "He outlined everything here. When I first saw them I read them over and over again, wondering why he would go through all the trouble to write this down if he didn't really have intentions to see it through."

"Okay, wait a minute, slow down. I don't understand," Morgan told him.

"After my father's attorney read his will, me and my siblings split the money and sold his house in Syracuse. None of us wanted it. I had everything from the house put into storage until one of us felt like dealing with it. There were two cars, a truck and a sedan. His will said he wanted them donated to the Pediatric Cancer Foundation in Richmond. He was born there and he had a twin brother who died from leukemia when they were three. Then I came here to sell the last properties he owned. We just wanted to be done with everything that concerned him as quickly as we could."

"Okay," she said, trying to follow the conversation and relate it to the huge sums of money she read on the statements she held. "So if you already split the money, sold the properties, put his belongings in storage, what is this?"

Gray smiled then. A huge smile that touched his eyes and squeezed Morgan's heart.

"My father was a simple man. One of the things I remember about him was that he didn't like flashy cars or clothes. When we were on television there were lots of offers for endorsements. Companies would send boxes and boxes of clothes and toys and things. Dad sent them all back. The paycheck from the show was all we needed. That's what my mother told us. That's one of the reasons she couldn't understand why my dad had suddenly fallen for the glamorous producer and walked away from his family."

He shook his head.

"After he was gone and they divorced, Dad started doing something he'd always loved—building things. He built engines and he turned that into a profitable business. My mother never had to fight him about child support because he always paid and sent gifts on our birthday and Christmas. He also sent us clothes at the beginning of the school year. He had bought a house in Syracuse—a modest house—and the two cars. Everything else, every other dime he made, he'd put into seven accounts in a bank on Grand Cayman Island."

Morgan was beginning to understand now.

"He saved money for each of us and for this town," Gray told her. "It was his intention to give back to the town that had given him his family."

She looked down at the statements again and shook her

head the same way Gray had just done. It was incredible and astonishing, and it made Gray extremely happy. For Morgan, surprisingly, that was enough. She stepped over the papers on the floor and went to him, wrapping her arms around him and hugging him tight.

Gray hugged her even tighter, burying his face in the crook of her neck.

"All these years," he said, "I wanted to hate him. He left us and we didn't know why. We thought he didn't love my mother, or us, enough to stay. As I grew older I just thought he was an ass and I didn't want anything to do with him. But while I wanted nothing to do with him, all he thought about was us the entire time he was gone."

Morgan nodded. "Yes, he did. He was determined to take care of you and your brothers and sisters, even when he was gone."

Gray pulled back. "And this town. He loved Temptation and all that the town had brought him."

"It seems he did," Morgan said, still holding the folder. "He loved the town a lot." A nervous giggle escaped as she recalled the 6.8 million-dollar sum in the account marked The Taylors of Temptation, LLC.

"He did," Gray said with a nod. "He absolutely did love this town, and you know what?"

"What?" she asked as Gray slipped the file from her hand and dropped it to the floor.

"I can see why he did. I can see why this small town of Temptation was so alluring to him."

"You can—" Her words were cut short when Gray grasped the nape of her neck, pulling her lips to his for a scorching-hot kiss.

He was devouring her and she loved it, loved the feel of his fingers scraping over her scalp as he tilted her head for deeper access. The other hand, strong, gripped her bottom, pressing her closer to his already thick arousal.

"Since day one," he murmured against her lips, "it's been you. Not this town, but you."

Morgan heard his words, even over the wild beating of her heart. She wrapped her arms tightly around his neck in an effort to hold him as close to her as she possibly could. Gray apparently wanted the same thing. As he turned, he lifted her up so that her legs wrapped quickly around his waist.

"Now you're all I think about," Gray said before thrusting his tongue deep into her mouth once more.

Morgan accepted his kiss and luxuriated in the heated sensations moving swiftly throughout her body. The sound of his voice, the touch of his hands, his mouth. Everything about him, about this moment was like a drug and she was deathly afraid that she was addicted. So much for drawing a line between them.

He walked them over to the bed then, keeping her in his arms as he reached behind him to push everything on top of the comforter onto the floor. He lowered her to the bed, yanking her sweater over her head, then hastily undid her pants and pushed them down her legs. When they stopped at her boots, Gray pulled them off quickly, tossing them across the room. Morgan undressed him as well, as anxious to feel him completely as he was to feel her.

"Since day one," she said, repeating his words, "it's been this way since day one." And there was no denying that now.

"Yes," he murmured, now naked, as he came over her, lifting her legs to once again lock behind his back. "Just you," Gray said, sinking his rigid length slowly, but most deliciously, inside of her.

Morgan trembled, her blunt-tipped nails digging into the skin of his shoulder. "Just you."

He moved much slower than she'd anticipated, which made the moment that much more intense. This was the moment she knew she had fallen. She'd wondered in the past few days, thought it was a fantasy, that it could ever happen this way, this quickly. Hell, she'd been in love before so Morgan was certain she knew how it felt. She was so damn wrong.

They rolled over the bed, Gray holding her tightly as she came up over him, continuing their slow ride to pleasure. When he sat up, too, holding her closely and kissing her mouth eagerly, she whimpered. This emotion was so much stronger and gripped her heart until she thought she might choke.

"I don't do relationships," he whispered in her ear. "You don't want this."

Morgan shook her head. "No," she sighed. "I don't."

He moved and she moved, their bodies joined to the hilt. He was thick and hot inside of her, filling physical and mental places she'd never even known existed.

"Yes," he whispered again, his hands going from her back, down to cup her bottom. "Yes, Morgan. Yes!"

She was shaking her head, her legs and arms trembling. His voice echoed in her head. His laughter, his smile, his words.

"Yes," she said, repeating him. "Yes, Gray. Yes!"

This plunge was different than before. Not like she'd fallen off a cliff to bliss, but as if she'd decided in that moment to make the jump. "Gray!" she yelled as every part of her shivered and shook with the intense release that claimed her.

He was right behind her, holding her tightly as his erection throbbed deep inside of her. He kissed her then, swallowing her cries into his own, until they both went still, only their hearts beating.

"Sonofabitch!" Kym screeched the moment she stepped inside Gray's room.

He moved quickly, pushing Morgan away from him and

pulling the comforter over to cover her nakedness. As for the fact that he, too, was naked, Gray didn't really care. He was much more concerned with his assistant, who had just barged into his room without calling or knocking first.

"What are you doing?" he asked as he got off the bed and reached for his jeans.

"Apparently, not as much as you are," Kym quipped. "I heard the rumors flying around, but you know, it's a small town so you never know what to believe. Besides, I didn't think you would ever sink so low."

Kym gasped and pointed to where Morgan still sat on the bed. "Her? Really, Grayson? You're choosing her?"

"You're out of line," Gray told her once he had his pants buttoned. "You've been out of line for weeks. I want you to leave this town today and get back to the office."

"She's a small-town slut!" Kym continued. "Looking for a daddy to her bratty children."

"Now you wait a minute," Morgan said, climbing off the bed, the comforter still wrapped around her. "You are not going to talk to me or about my children like that."

"Shut up!" Kym yelled at her. "You're stupid, too. How can you be tasked with teaching children when you're so damn stupid? He's not in love with you. This isn't some rags-to-riches story, sweetie. He's a millionaire. He doesn't belong in this sorry town and he certainly won't stay here with you, no matter how much you put out."

Gray didn't see it coming. He would have never in his wildest dreams thought it would happen right in front of him, but it did. Morgan punched Kym so hard in the face that Kym fell flat on her ass, onto the pile of papers Gray had been reading just an hour ago.

"I'm pressing charges," Kym immediately squealed as she tried to get up.

Gray looked at Morgan to make sure she was all right.

She wasn't even breathing hard. He resisted the urge to smile and moved to help Kym up from the floor.

"I want her in jail, Grayson. She needs to be behind bars and then we'll get out of this dirty little town," she continued.

"No," he said simply. "You're going back to Miami. Today. And if I hear one word about you talking to the cops, you're going to be sorry you ever met me."

Now on her feet, Kym wrenched her arm free of his grasp and looked at him with pure anger bubbling in her eyes. "I already do," she told him before turning and walking out of the room.

"She's going to sue you for wrongful discharge," Morgan said from behind him.

He'd been watching the open doorway, feeling the brisk cold of the evening against his bare chest and wondering how he'd come to be here in this place and in this predicament. Six months ago he was in Dubai brokering yet another lucrative business deal. He was sleeping in penthouse suites and sipping fifty-thousand-dollar bottles of champagne. Now, he was staying on a horse farm, wearing jeans and freezing his ass off.

"She can't," he said as he moved to close the door. "She's an at-will employee. Meaning she's there at my will. I have the sole authority to fire her without cause or notice. My employee handbook is clear and airtight, as per my attorney, who is on a monthly retainer."

She'd pulled on her jeans by then, and her sweater, alerting Gray to the fact that she'd thrown that punch while wrapped only in a comforter. How was that for sexy?

Morgan ran her fingers through the top of her hair.

Gray moved closer to her, taking her hand and kissing her slightly bruised knuckles.

Chapter 12

Christmas Eve

Today was going to be a busy day. Not that the last couple of days hadn't been, Morgan thought as she sipped on her second cup of coffee. Wendy had already picked up the children and they were doing what her sister called the best type of shopping—the last-minute kind. They were all going to meet at the community center at four o'clock this afternoon. Before then, Morgan needed to wrap her own gifts, clean her house and make sure everything was in line for the play that night. That meant she needed to go to the center and check on all the props, the programs and the lights, and had to call Mrs. Reed to see if she required any assistance with the food.

Yes, Morgan thought, she needed this second cup of coffee, and possibly a clone to get through this day. That thought had her smiling and shaking her head. She realized she wouldn't want her life any other way. She loved the tasks she was responsible for in Temptation, and loved the thought of all the pleased faces once the play was finally being performed. Tomorrow would be Christmas, the first Christmas where the children would have her and Gray…and the barrage of toys he'd purchased for them.

Morgan still couldn't believe all the stuff that was delivered to Gray's room at the farm. The train set that Jack had been begging her for all year long and the baby doll that looked like a real child that Lily insisted she needed to complete her five-year-old life. Plus so much more. He'd also bought clothes, shoes and coats for them. It was too much, Morgan knew, and she'd attempted to tell him the same.

"Nothing is too much for them," he'd told her. "This is the only time in their entire lives that the most important thing will be the promise Santa keeps. It's a magical time of wishes and expectations, cheer and excitement. I want that for them. The same way I had it, I want Jack and Lily to have the same."

She'd stopped the argument then because the mere fact that this man wanted so much for her children left her speechless. There was a lot about Gray that had left her without words or explanations lately. She'd enjoyed thinking about him about as much as she enjoyed being with him, which was part of the reason she almost didn't hear the knock on her door.

Morgan put down her cup and made her way to the door, then pulled it open without looking through the peephole to see who it was. A part of her had thought—hoped—it was Gray. That part was sadly mistaken.

"Happy Christmas Eve," Harry said, a huge grin on his face.

Morgan heard his voice but it took her a moment to realize he was down on his knees.

"Happy Christmas Eve, Harry. What are you doing?" she asked, pulling her robe closed tighter around her.

Harry reached for her hand, holding it tightly in his. "I wanted to do this right now before things got too hectic today," he told her.

"Harry," she began, hating the sick feeling creeping in the pit of her stomach.

"No. Please don't interrupt me," he said. "I've been practicing this for years but I'm still as nervous as a school-boy."

Harry chuckled and Morgan shook her head. "But Harry, I don't think—"

"Right," he said, reaching into his coat pocket. "I don't want you to think. Not just yet anyway. Let me just get this out."

"But—" Morgan tried again to stop him.

"Morgan Ann Langston Hill," he began loudly. "I swear I've been in love with you since the sixth-grade dance when you brought me that cup of water after I choked on those dry, stale crackers."

She remembered that day and now she couldn't help but think it might have been easier to simply let him choke. Surely, someone else would have saved him. Maybe Patsy Glenn would have done the honors. Then Harry would be at Patsy's doorstep right now making a fool out of himself, instead of at Morgan's.

"I can't think of any other woman but you. I didn't have anything to offer you when we were young. You went away to college and I vowed that I'd have my own place and my own business started by the time you returned. That way I could take care of you, of us and our family. Then you came back and got married before I could even get over here to see you." Harry sighed.

"I watched you all those years with him and then you had his babies and I just wanted to die. But I didn't and he did and I thought, 'Thank You, Lord. Thank You. Thank You. Thank You.' I knew it was my time. But I had to let you grieve. I've always been slow. My daddy says that all the time. Anyway, I'm not moving slow anymore. Morgan, I'm asking you to be my wife."

With one hand Harry popped open the little black box. There was a diamond staring back at her, like an eye judging her for allowing him to get this far when she already knew what her answer was.

"Harry…" she began.

He shook his head. "No. I want you to take a few minutes. Inhale the crisp Christmas Eve air and think about all that we've been through and all that we can be to each other. I can adopt the twins. You can move into my place or I can move in here until we find something bigger. We can be a family, Morgan, just like we've both always wanted."

She had wanted a family and for a while Morgan had thought it would be with a man from Temptation. That notion had been dispelled when she'd married James. Now, she had this guy who had been born and raised here. Harry had roots here, he loved this town and he wasn't going anywhere. That's exactly what Morgan always thought she wanted. Until Gray.

"No, Harry. I'm sorry, but I cannot marry you," she told him.

The words seemed cold, or was it the breeze that had decided to blow at just that moment?

Harry shot to his feet instantly.

"You didn't think about it long enough," he said. "Let's go inside. Maybe you're too cold to think."

"No, it's not that," Morgan said even as Harry stepped toward her.

She stepped back, letting him into her house.

"Harry, I've always thought of you as a good friend," Morgan began. This had to be done and it had to be done right now. Harry needed to know that he should move on without her.

"I'm not in love with you," she said simply.

"But we're good friends," Harry said, looking at her as if he was really trying to understand her words. "A husband and wife should be good friends."

"We are," she told him. "And I know that a married couple should have a friendship. But that's not enough, Harry. Not for me or for you. There should be love. You should love your wife above all else and cherish her."

"I've cherished you for so long, Morgan. And I shouldn't have waited. I'm so sorry, I shouldn't have waited."

He moved closer and Morgan took another step back. She didn't like how Harry was looking at her.

"I won't wait any longer, Morgan. I won't let you make us wait," he said as he reached out and grabbed her by the arms.

"Let go of me," she said, trying to remain calm.

"No," Harry insisted. "Not this time."

"I'm serious, Harry, let me go!"

Instead, Harry grasped her arms tightly and lifted her right off her feet before pushing her back until she slammed into the wall. "I'm not going to let you go. Not. Again!" he screamed into her face.

Then Morgan felt like she was sliding. Harry's grip on her was quickly released and before she could speak she was sliding down the wall to her knees.

"I believe the lady answered your question," Gray yelled at Harry.

Harry was now on the floor beside Morgan's broken coffee table, where Gray had tossed him across the room.

"You!" Harry blurted, quickly coming to his feet.

Morgan stood as well. She had déjà vu, only with a different cast of characters. Knowing how the previous incident had ended, she hurried over to stand in front of Gray.

"Harry, I want you out of my house before I call Sheriff Duncan over here and have you arrested for assault. That would ruin your mother's Christmas, now wouldn't it?" she shouted at him.

"He doesn't love you!" Harry yelled. "He's just using you! I know it, half the town knows it! Hell, his assistant, who's known him forever, knows it. You're the only one too blind to see it."

"I want you to go," Morgan said, trying valiantly to ignore his words.

"You heard her," Gray insisted. "Get out and don't come back."

"I'll do whatever I damn well please," Harry shouted back, but he moved toward the door.

"Not to her and not anymore," Gray continued. He moved toward the door as well. "This is the last time I'll see you here."

"Oh, yeah?" Harry asked as he stepped to Gray.

"Yes," Gray answered without hesitation as he stepped toward Harry. "Don't let the suit fool you," Gray warned. "I'll break your jaw before you can throw the first punch and that'll only be the beginning."

There was something sexy about those words, spoken so icily and coming from a man dressed in a designer black suit. He looked formidable, almost like those gangsters in mob stories. His tone sounded deadly enough that it wouldn't have surprised Morgan one bit if he'd reached behind his back and pulled a gun from the band of his pants.

Harry must have thought the same thing, or something in that neighborhood, because he backed away so quickly he almost fell through the door.

"You're gonna be sorry," Harry continued, still yelling as he walked to his truck. "When he breaks your heart, Morgan, you're gonna be so sorry you let me walk away.

And I'm not gonna let you back in. Even when you're crying and sorry, I won't!"

Harry pulled off with a screech of tires and Morgan slammed the door. She leaned into it, letting her head fall as she wondered how the hell she'd missed Harry's true feelings for her. If she'd cut him off earlier, years ago, this would have never happened.

"Hey," Gray said, touching a finger to her chin and lifting her head until she was staring up at him. "He's a fool."

She began shaking her head. "No. He's not. He was just in love with me."

"No," Gray told her simply. "If he was truly in love with you he would beg, steal, tear down walls and climb mountains to keep you."

Morgan didn't know what to say to that. She didn't know what had made Gray say it and she was too afraid to ask. Instead, she accepted his hug and the warmth of his sweet kiss. She did not, however, contemplate the words that Harry said about Gray using her, or the fact that Kym had basically said the same thing. She wouldn't think about what might possibly happen between her and Gray in the future. Not right now.

"Let it be Christmas every day!" Ethan shouted, a huge grin spread across his face.

Arielle Beaumont, who played Tiny Tim, simply shook her head. They'd spent three hours yesterday going over this part. Morgan had corrected Ethan at least four times, telling him the line was "I will keep Christmas in my heart," but Ethan, true to form, did his own thing.

"God bless us, every one," Arielle stated, her voice loud and clear over the chuckles that had begun.

The stagehands, Lenny and John Petrie, pulled on the curtains until they closed completely and the crowd continued to clap. Morgan let out a deep breath. It felt like she'd been holding it in for the last four hours, when final preparations for this evening's event had kicked off.

Mayor Pullum took the stage then, with Rayford Malloy standing proudly beside her. Rayford's chest remained poked out—he was proud of his son for making a mockery of the play with his original lines and gestures.

"We want to give a hearty thanks to Morgan Hill and her first-grade class for bringing Charles Dickens's timeless classic to a whole new life here in Temptation. It was truly a wonderful time," Mayor Pullum enthused.

More applause and Morgan smiled as she hurried to the back, where Wendy and Granny were helping to get the children undressed. There would be mingling and refreshments for probably another half hour. Nana Lou and her daughter, Pam, were in the front hall of the community center, where they'd cleaned up after the potluck dinner and now had cake, cider and coffee prepared.

As for Morgan's part in Temptation's annual holiday extravaganza, it was done. Now she was looking forward to a hot bath and quiet Christmas Eve with her twins. Tomorrow would be breakfast after the children enjoyed their gifts and then dinner at Granny's. She was due at her grandmother's house at noon to help with the cooking and preparations and Morgan was really looking forward to spending that time with her family. These were the people she knew and was sure of, unlike Harry. And Gray.

All day long Morgan had attempted to put the memories of what had happened at her place with Harry and Gray out of her mind. Just five days ago she'd been seen naked by Gray's assistant, the woman she'd ultimately had to punch in the face for running her mouth about Morgan's children. Then the confrontation with Harry that Morgan was sure could have gotten more out of hand if Harry hadn't come to his last bit of sense and left her house when Gray told him to.

Morgan didn't know what was going on. When did her quiet and routine life get turned upside down by rude and delusional people? The moment Gray Taylor waltzed back into town was the undeniable answer.

"He's making a statement." Wendy tugged on Morgan's arm. "Come on, we gotta get up front so we can hear him."

Morgan had just arrived in the back room, only to see that the children were already dressed in their regular clothes and headed toward the foyer with their happy chatter.

"Come on!" Wendy insisted.

Morgan followed her sister with tired feet and a headache she'd been praying would stay tamped down until she got home. That probably wasn't going to happen, Morgan thought as she stepped into the auditorium once more to see Gray standing on the stage where Mayor Pullum had been.

"I know that some of you have wondered why I've been here for just about a month now," he said.

He looked really good, as always, wearing gray slacks, a gray shirt and cheerful red tie. Morgan had gotten used to seeing him in his casual clothes these last couple of weeks, but nothing beat the sight of this man in dress clothes. He took her breath away every time. Tonight, she couldn't resist the small smile as she noticed he was wearing the tie that Jack and Lily had insisted Morgan buy when they were out gift shopping earlier in the week. It was all red, but at the bottom there was a wintry scene with two snowmen having a snowball fight.

"It's just like when we played in the snow and built George," Jack had said as he stood in the store holding it up proudly.

"Yup, it is. It's a memory!" Lily had added with her own excitement at having participated in finding the perfect gift for Gray.

To Morgan's surprise and relief, Gray had been elated to receive the early gift from the children and had promised to wear it tonight. Morgan wasn't sure how she felt about him making promises to her children, even if he did keep them. No, that wasn't totally true. She was sure it made her feel wonderfully warm on the inside, her heart near to bursting with joy. She just didn't know if it was safe to like that feeling so much.

"I decided that to make an informed decision about whether or not to sell this building and the hospital that I needed to get to know the town of Temptation once more," Gray continued. "When I left this town I was only a child. This used to be home, only it wasn't as happy and wonderful as some of you may have thought. In these past weeks, however, I've experienced more change than I think I have in my entire adult life. I owe that to some pretty special people."

Morgan's cheeks burned with embarrassment as some of the adults looked to her. Wendy did a quiet hand clap in Morgan's direction because she was all for giving people in town something to talk about.

"Let them gossip, girl," she'd told Morgan after Morgan had shared what happened with Kym in Gray's room. "That's what they do around here. No sense in you or anybody else trying to change that. At least they're gossiping about you and a good man, instead of some deadbeat."

As usual Morgan hadn't thought of things that way, but leave it to Wendy to put her own slant on a situation. Morgan added that to all the things her big sister did better than her.

"I'm not sure how all of you collectively will feel about my decision, but I've decided that tonight would be the best night to announce my plans," Gray said.

The room went completely quiet at that moment and Morgan touched a hand to her stomach, which immediately had butterflies flipping and flopping around. She was just clearing her throat when she saw Jack and Lily run up on the stage with Gray.

"What are they doing?" she whispered and then made a motion to go and get them.

"Let them be," Granny said, touching a hand to Morgan's arm. "They wanted to be with him and I let 'em."

"But it's rude, Granny. He's up there talking and look at them," Morgan stated as she looked back at her grandmother and then up to the stage, where Gray had already picked up Lily, planting her on his side. Lily dutifully lay her head on his shoulder, while Jack stood right beside Gray as if he was attached to his leg.

There were a few chuckles as Gray said, "Thanks for the help you two," and grinned wildly.

"My father had plans to return to Temptation," Gray continued. "He wanted to come back and finish helping the town that had given him his family. So in that vein, I will not be selling the hospital. I will be renovating it and adding on The Taylor Generational Wing, which will focus on obstetrics and fertility studies."

There was immediate applause and Granny laced her fingers with Morgan's. But she didn't look to her grandmother—her gaze was trained on Gray.

"In addition to the hospital," he said over the low murmurs, "I will also be renovating the community center. This facility can serve such a bigger function here in Temptation and I'd like to see it flourish. One of the main updates to the center will be a separate theater center, where professional plays can be put on for the public."

If Morgan had been blushing before, she was about to full-on gush now, as Gray stated the idea she'd given him for the community center's use.

"It took a while to figure this out, but Temptation will always be home to the Taylors, and a family should always take care of home," Gray said. "I wish the town of Temptation and all of you a very merry Christmas and a happy start to the New Year."

He walked off the stage with Jack and Lily in tow, just as Millie hurried over to where Granny, Wendy and Morgan were standing.

"You did it!" Millie said to Morgan. "Hot damn, Ida Mae, she did it!"

Millie pulled Morgan to her for a quick hug. Behind her, Fred grinned.

"Yes, I must say we're in for some big changes here in town and we owe that all to you, Morgan," Fred said.

Morgan was already shaking her head. "No. You're mistaken. This was Gray's decision, I had nothing to do with it."

"Oh, Ida Mae, this girl here is something," Millie told Granny. "She doesn't know a thing about a woman's power, does she? But I knew it all along. Ever since I saw you two together at the charity ball. I knew you would be the one to turn him around. That's why Fred and I gave you all that information. We knew you would help save our town."

"But I didn't," Morgan responded.

"Just smile and say it's wonderful, Morgan," Granny said.

Wendy agreed with their grandmother's declarations as she leaned in to whisper in Morgan's ear. "That's right, just smile. This town's going to be kissing your ass for years to come for this."

Morgan didn't want anybody kissing her ass and she didn't want to take credit for something she didn't do, but just about an hour and a half later, as she walked into her house, she heard Gray say the same thing.

"None of this would have been possible without you," he stated.

Jack and Lily had gone into their bedroom to change

into their pajamas. The Christmas tree was lit in the living room, presents underneath. The house still smelled like the cookies Morgan and the kids had baked yesterday and the pine candle that Granny had given her when she'd complained about Morgan not having a real tree.

"You made the decision that was right for you and your family, Gray. Your father had those plans long before I came along. I won't take responsibility for a conclusion you came to on your own," she told him.

He shook his head. "If you hadn't insisted I look at those buildings, I wouldn't have. Then I would have never found out about what my father had planned all these years. I wouldn't have learned more about a man I thought I never wanted to know."

Morgan took a deep breath and let it out slowly. "I don't know what's going on anymore," she admitted. "Things have just been going so fast. One minute I'm going along with life as usual and the next you're here and I'm showing you buildings like I'm some real estate agent and you're making snowmen with my kids."

He'd come to stand close to her then. "You forgot the part about the great sex," he said with that grin that never failed to warm her.

She shook her head. "I don't think either one of us can forget that."

"Not on your life," he said, reaching out to touch a finger to her chin. "It's good, Morgan. All of this feels right. I didn't expect it, either. It's not something I planned or would have even believed if somebody had told me this was where I'd be one year ago."

"No," Morgan told him with a tilt of her head. "You thought you'd be in Miami, maybe going to a corporate holiday party, or perhaps you would have taken a trip for the holidays. You'd lie on some beach all Christmas Eve and then spend a very quiet Christmas with room service."

The thought sounded lonely to her, but it was exactly how she pictured Gray's holiday celebrations.

He shrugged. "Sometimes I think you know me better than I know myself."

She didn't know what to say to that.

"But this is so much better, Morgan. This is more of what my mother would have wanted for me, for all of her children. I'm a little tired after helping Fred, Lenny and John with the final setup for tonight. Discovering that half the chairs in the hall were broken and having to transport ones from the hospital in the Porsche was a little grueling. But I loved every second of it," he told her.

"Yeah, Nana Lou was pissed that Harry didn't show up like he'd promised," she said and then frowned.

"Don't do that," he told her with a shake of his head. "That's not your fault. Harry Reed is a grown man. Grown men get rejected by women every day. It's been happening since the beginning of time. There's no excuse to act like a jealous ass."

Morgan knew that but it didn't mean she couldn't feel bad about how things had turned out. "I'm too tired to argue," she said with a little chuckle.

Jack and Lily came running out at that moment.

"Can we open one gift tonight?" Jack asked.

"Yes, Mama, can we?" Lily begged.

Morgan shook her head. "Now, you know we open gifts on Christmas morning after Santa comes."

"That's the old way, though," Lily continued. "Can't we do something new?"

"Yeah, like we built a snowman and named him George. We didn't do that last year. So this should be the year of new stuff," Jack added.

"That's right, we should. Right, Mr. Gray?" Lily asked.

Then her daughter leaned over to whisper—which was very loud because at five years old, Lily had not perfected her inside voice. "We asked the right way, didn't we? That's what you told us to say, right?"

Morgan looked at Gray, who instantly looked away from Lily and then grinned. "You did it perfectly. Both of you should have had bigger parts in the play, instead of just being the children playing in the street."

"So this was an audition for them to be in next year's play?" Morgan asked skeptically.

Gray shook his head and moved over to the tree. He reached down and retrieved a slim box.

"No. I just had this idea that since I was doing something new this year, that maybe we all should," he said before reaching out to hand her the box. "Merry Christmas, Morgan."

She didn't take the box. In fact, Morgan had slipped her arms behind her back, where her hands were now clenched together.

"Open it, Mama," Jack told her. "Open it so we can see what he got for you!"

Her son was bouncing from one foot to the other, always the impatient one, she thought as she tried to ignore the rapid beating of her heart. When Morgan realized that Gray intended to stay for Christmas she'd known she had to get him a gift, from the kids, of course. They'd picked out socks and a Temptation T-shirt so that he'd remember them when he returned to Miami. It was a simple gift, one that she would have purchased for any friend. Only there hadn't been a male friend in Morgan's life to buy gifts for in a very long time.

"Take it, Mama. It's rude to give a gift back," Lily said, interrupting her thoughts.

Morgan had told her daughter this same thing when Bert Valley had given Lily a live frog for her birthday last year.

"Take it, Morgan," Gray said. "I want you to have this."

With hands that betrayed her, as they shook and showed

how nervous she was feeling, Morgan took the box. She saw her kids watching her expectantly, so she shook it and they laughed, as she knew they would.

"You can't guess what it is like that. You gotta open it," Jack told her with another giggle.

"Well, maybe I should sit down first," Morgan said, trying to buy time and to get off her feet because her knees felt wobbly.

"Come on," Gray said as he helped her over to the couch.

"You're loving this, aren't you?" she said, looking up at him, unable to keep her own grin at bay.

"It's great," he told her. "Just like you."

Her stomach did another flip-flop and Morgan dropped onto the couch. She hurriedly opened the box because having three sets of eyes on her in anticipation was more pressure than worrying about whether or not she should be taking gifts from Gray. That worry was magnified when she finally lifted the top of the box to see the sparkle of blue sapphires glinting in the lights from the Christmas tree.

"Gray," she whispered. "This is way too much."

"It was in the envelope," he told her. "The one my father left with my name on it. He'd planned to give it to my mother that year for their anniversary. The year he left."

Morgan shook her head and pushed the box back toward him. "I can't take this. It belongs to you and your family. I can't."

"You can because I'm giving it to you," he told her, reaching down to take the necklace out of the box.

"It's so pretty," Lily exclaimed. "Shiny and pretty and your favorite color is blue, Mama."

"You should have gotten her a deck of cards," Jack said with an unimpressed look on his face. "She likes to play solitaire more than she wears fancy stuff."

Jack was right—Morgan never went anywhere that she

could wear something like this. She was about to use that as her excuse for giving it back to Gray when her house phone rang. Saved by the bell, she thought as she hurriedly moved away from Gray, who had been waiting to put the necklace on her.

"Hello?" she answered. "What? When? How?" she asked, her heart thumping wildly. "...Right...Fine. Get here fast!"

"What is it?" Gray asked the moment she turned around.

"That was Wendy," she said, still clutching the phone. "The community center is on fire."

Chapter 13

It was gone.

As Gray stepped out of his car and raced across the street to follow Morgan, he knew the moment they were stopped by police officers. Morgan gasped, covering her mouth with her hands, her head shaking as tears filled her eyes. Inside Gray raged, but he put a steady arm around Morgan and held her close.

The sight was unlike anything he'd ever seen before. Black smoke billowing up into the night sky, bright and angry flames licking over what was left of the building's structure, destroying everything in their wake.

"It's too hot to put out right now, Mr. Taylor," a man dressed in a fireman's uniform said as he came to stand beside Gray.

"Call me Gray," he said to the man, who nodded.

"I'm Chief Alderson. But call me Dave."

"I want to know what caused this fire as soon as you know, Dave," Gray told him.

Dave nodded once more, his solemn gaze focused on the fire, just as Gray's remained.

"It's damn hot in there. I pulled my men out after about ten minutes. We couldn't get past the first thirty feet inside. Offhand, I'd say some sort of accelerant," Dave reported.

The man had said the last sentence in a hushed tone and he'd leaned in a little closer to Gray as he spoke. Morgan was on Gray's other side and with the noise of the fire and the people still coming onto the scene, Gray hoped she hadn't heard what Dave had said. Gray, however, clenched his teeth in anger.

"Oh, my lord, it's burning," Millie said as she came running over to them. "What could have happened?"

Morgan had shifted so that she now faced Millie and Fred, who were standing close.

"You turned off everything when you left, didn't you?" Millie instantly questioned Morgan.

"Of course I did," Morgan replied with much irritation, rightfully so.

Gray looked at Millie with only partial disbelief. He'd been around town for weeks and in that time he'd watched Millie talk friendly with some townspeople and in the next instant cut them close with her sharp tongue. She was a force to be reckoned with, someone that most citizens of the town did their best to steer clear of. Gray had no intention of being like the majority.

"We checked everything before we left, Millie. Even that faulty fuse box in the basement. Fred, you're paid a monthly fee to manage this property. When was the last time you had the electrical wiring checked?" Gray asked.

"Now look here, you can't come here and start accusing my husband. We take our jobs and life in this town seriously, Gray," Millie insisted.

Fred was nodding beside his wife. "I got some reports

that there was a problem. Harry told me he'd been over to fix it a couple of times so I thought it was fine."

As if hearing his name had conjured his presence, Harry walked up. Gray wasn't thrilled to see the guy, but he definitely was not prepared to see Kym walking right beside him. Gray hadn't seen her in days and had presumed she'd left town like he'd told her to do.

"I did check out the fuse box and like I told you last month, it was fine," Harry said, his angry glare toward Gray evident.

"The power went out again a month ago," Morgan said, more to Gray than to anyone else.

He nodded. "I remember. The first night I was in town I had to go down and flip the fuse for the power to switch back on," Gray said.

"I can't fix a problem I didn't know about," Harry insisted. "Maybe if you'd called me instead of letting this suit-and-tie guy try to meddle in things that weren't his business, this could have been prevented."

"Hold on, everyone," Dave interjected. "I haven't given a cause for this fire yet. So let's put a cap on all this blame you're tossing around. Now, I'm gonna have to ask that you all go home, or get across the street because the building's frame is gonna start breaking off any minute now."

Morgan looked over to the building, shaking her head once more. "I can't believe this," she said. "After all the worrying and contemplating what you were going to do with this building and now it's just gone."

"When one building goes, you build another," Kym quipped. "I know of two developers who would love this spot. You know them, too, don't you, Millie?"

At Kym's words both Gray and Morgan looked to Millie to see what her response would be.

"You ten-cent whore!" Millie spat. "I warned you not to come to my town with your drama. Yet you're still here and now you have the nerve to push this in my direction."

Within the next second, Millie was lunging for Kym. Fred and Gray both held her back while Kym stood with a sickening smirk on her face.

"Just tell them that you've been in touch with the developers trying to see how much money the town could make off the strip mall they want to build. Tell them how you were against the idea at first, but when one of the developers suggested that maybe Fred would be interested in managing the rental and maintenance of the outlet mall they proposed, your eyes turned from shifty brown to greedy green."

Millie tried to go after her again and this time, Morgan stepped closer to Kym.

"Why don't you just leave town. You don't like it here and you obviously don't like the people. So it would make all the sense in the world for you to go back where you came from," Morgan told her.

"It would make all the sense in the world for you to grow a brain," Kym stated.

Harry stood right beside her, looking as if he agreed with every ridiculous word that Kym said. For the first time in his life Gray wanted to physically harm someone.

"Let's go," he said, touching a hand to Morgan's arm.

When she readily moved to stand beside him Gray could almost hear his mother's words echoing in his mind. *Jealousy and hatred are two emotions you can neither predict nor cure. Let the ones who suffer with it be, live your life in spite of.*

With a shake of his head and a last look at both of them, Gray walked Morgan to his car and helped her inside.

* * *

Morgan held on to Wendy as she cried when they returned to Morgan's house.

"It's going to be all right," Wendy told her. "Gray's going to rebuild, aren't you?"

He hadn't given it a second thought. "Definitely. We were planning to add an additional building onto the back side anyway. This way we'll do a completely new design. I know a wonderful and innovative architect that I can call as soon as the holiday is over. It's going to be bigger and better, without any doubt."

"See, it's all going to work out," Wendy said, pulling away from Morgan and giving Gray a grateful look. "As for that tramp and Harry's punk ass, they're going to get what's coming to them. You know Granny wholeheartedly believes in karma."

Morgan chuckled then as she wiped her eyes and Gray wanted nothing more than to hold her in his arms and tell her just what her sister had just told her. Everything was going to work out. He was going to make sure that it did.

When Wendy was gone, Morgan turned to Gray and said, "You know Granny also believes wholeheartedly in voodoo hexes and curses. I wouldn't put it past her to be in her house now mixing up some concoction to make sure Harry and Kym got just what they deserved for being spiteful."

"I'm not going to say that's a bad idea," Gray joked.

Morgan shook her head. Her stance was still tense, but a little smile came through. A very tired and weary one.

"Look, the children are asleep. It's late and you're tired. How about I run you a hot bath and put you to bed?"

She leaned against the closed door and sighed. "That sounds heavenly."

"Then it shall be done," Gray said immediately.

He went to the door, moved her gently to the side while he checked the locks and then walked her back toward the bathroom. While they walked he massaged her shoulders, hating all the tightness he felt there.

"Dave is going to find out how the fire started and we're going to rebuild. I don't want you to worry about any of that," he told her.

She remained silent while they moved into the bathroom. He turned on the water and waited until the temperature was right, then said, "Now, let's get you bathed and ready for bed."

She'd been staring at him, her arms folded over her chest. "I'm not one of the children, Gray. And I'm not one of your business deals that you're fixing."

He moved to stand in front of her. "Never mistook you for either," he said.

"This was exactly what I was afraid of all along," she said with a sigh. "I don't like this feeling and I know it sounds silly and probably unrealistic, but I don't like loss. It's just too heavy for me to deal with. My kids are at the community center all the time. When it wasn't this play it was arts-and-crafts night, or story time. There was always something there for them to do and now it's gone."

He cupped her cheek and shook his head. "That old building is gone," Gray told her. "There will be a new building and all those activities and many more will resume. Remember, you planned some of the things that will take place there. We can plan even more."

She was still shaking her head and when she looked up at him there were tears in her eyes once again. "The only thing that was here for me after James died was this town. That community center and the people there saved me plenty of nights when I thought I would go crazy with loneliness and the kids would hate me for being such a boring mother. This is exactly what I was afraid of when you first came to town. And I know that you said you're going to rebuild, I just still feel this sense of loss."

"Stop it," he said sternly, but not angrily. "I know about loss, too, Morgan. I lost my mother when all I ever knew was to count on her. I lost my father long before that and I still don't think I ever understood why. So I know all about that lonely feeling that grows so big and so heavy inside of you until you think there's no way you can take another breath. I know about not being sure what you'll do the next day and the day after that, because you've lost someone." He cupped both hands to her face now and stared intently into her eyes.

"But what I also know right now, standing in this space with you so close to me, is that I've never felt more complete in my life. The here and now is what's important. Nothing else. And I'm right here with you, right now. Jack and Lily are sleeping soundly in their beds waiting for Santa to drop off all their goodies and that tub is about to overflow with the hot bath you requested."

She smiled just as one tear slipped down her cheek. Gray caught it, wiping it away with his thumb, and smiled down at her.

"We're going to have a fabulous Christmas, something new and exciting for us all. We're not going to think about this mess with the fire or anything else that doesn't make us feel happy and content. Just for one day, we're going to do that."

He looked up at the ceiling and then back down to her. "I wish there was some mistletoe up there right now."

"Why? So you could kiss me and then get lucky? Taking advantage of an emotionally drained woman doesn't seem like your style, Mr. Gray," she told him jokingly.

Gray smiled. "I'm going to put you into this bathtub

and I'll take advantage of you later," he said before kissing her lips.

She kissed him back, wrapping her arms immediately around his neck and making Gray want to get into that tub with her. In fact, Gray thought in that moment that he wanted to do everything with this woman. Eat, talk, plan, pray every day—he wanted it all.

Chapter 14

Gray carried Lily into her grandmother's house, while Jack walked beside Morgan holding tight to the Spider-Man super car Gray had given him this morning.

"Merry Christmas!" Granny shouted the moment she walked into the hallway to see everyone taking off their coats.

"Merry Christmas!" the children replied as they ran and hugged her.

Gray turned to hand Morgan their coats, as she was standing near the closet and had just hung up her own.

"Merry Christmas," he said, and she turned just in time to see him locked in a tight hug with Granny.

Wendy came out next, an apron around her waist and an already exasperated look on her face.

"Merry Christmas, y'all," she said, bending down to hug the kids as they ran to her.

Granny pulled Morgan close for a hug after she'd hung

up the coats, which he'd finally given to her after his embrace with Granny.

"Stop looking so sad," Granny whispered in Morgan's ear. "It's Christmas, remember. Only happiness today."

Morgan nodded as she released her grandmother, but seeing Gray also hugging Wendy and laughing made her pause once more. They'd slept together again last night—no sex, just sleep. Gray held her all through the night, his arms wrapped tightly around her while Morgan had tried to fall asleep. She'd stared into the dark for longer than she cared to remember, thinking about all that had happened in just one month's time.

"Hey there, sis, you hanging in there?" Wendy asked as she came to stand in front of Morgan once Granny had returned to get Lily and Jack.

She was carting the children off into the living room, to open the gifts she'd bought for them, no doubt.

Shaking her head and taking a deep breath, then releasing it slowly, Morgan stared at her sister.

"I'm okay, I guess," she said.

"We're all going to be okay around here. It's about time Temptation stepped into the twenty-first century. I was thinking last night that Gray is just the person to propel us in that direction," Wendy told her.

Gray had gone into the living room, too, probably sensing that Morgan needed to be alone with her sister for a few minutes. He was like that, she thought, always knowing what she needed before she even verbalized her wishes. It was different having someone around to do that when for so long it seemed like she was the only one supplying needs in her household, putting her own on the back burner.

"But will he stay here to do that?" she asked Wendy. "Or will he go back to Miami, where his home, his business and his life is?"

"Wait," Wendy said, grabbing Morgan by the shoulders. "You're not asking just for the sake of the town, are you? You're thinking about you and him? Oh, my goodness, you're in love with him, aren't you?" Wendy squealed.

"Be quiet," Morgan said, waving a hand at her sister and looking toward the living room. "What's the point in waiting until we're alone to have a conversation if you're just going to shout out what we're talking about?"

"Oh my, oh my!" Wendy said, stepping from one foot to the other like an excited child. "Morgan's in love. She's really in love!"

Wendy had spoken in a more hushed tone this time. Morgan frowned.

"I was in love before, with my husband, remember?" she said to Wendy. Even though, to be quite honest, Morgan hadn't thought about her marriage or her relationship with James in the last couple of weeks.

In the beginning, when Gray was here and after the first time they'd had sex, she had thought about James a lot. Reconciling with herself over the fact that there was now another man in her life, she figured. But since then, her only thoughts of James had been regarding the children and what it would mean to them to have a man around who wasn't their biological father. Which brought her right back to the question she'd asked Wendy—was Gray going to stay in Temptation with them?

Wendy nodded. "I'm not saying you weren't. But for so long you've been acting like your life only revolves around the kids. I mean, hell, you haven't even been dressing like you used to."

Morgan immediately looked down at her black jeans, leather knee-length boots and red-and-white holiday sweater.

"I think I look just fine," she replied.

"Yeah, but before you met James, you looked fabulous.

All the time. I mean, you wore dresses and sexy blouses. You had longer hair and did your makeup."

"I like my hair short, it's easier to manage. And makeup in Temptation is like snow in July—absolutely out of place," Morgan quipped.

Wendy shook her head. "Not true. I put on my face every day, no matter what. And there are dozens of other women living here that do the same. You just adopted all these new rules once you became a widow. But now you're in love again and you and the kids can have a complete family. I think it's fantastic."

"Ah, excuse me, but your grandmother sent me out here to collect you two. She said it's time to open gifts," Gray said.

Morgan instantly froze at the sight of him, praying he hadn't heard their conversation, especially the parts from Wendy because apparently her inside voice was still disabled.

"We're coming," Wendy said happily and started walking toward the living room.

Gray looked at Morgan. "Everything all right?" he asked.

Morgan fixed a smile on her face and replied, "Everything's fine." She headed into the living room, hoping and praying that things would be fine in the end. Although she still wasn't quite sure.

Gray was overwhelmed.

"Go on and open it, stop being so silly," Granny told him after the second box had been set in front of him.

At Morgan's place this morning, the children had presented him with another gift. Leather slippers because Jack said his mother insisted everyone wear slippers in the house and each time Gray had stayed over, he'd only walked around in his socks. Morgan had also given him a gift—a book on vintage cars because he'd told her about his hobby of looking at the cars, but had never bought one.

"You should have a hobby," she'd told him. "Something to occupy your mind other than work."

Gray almost told her that there was *someone* who had been occupying his mind more than work lately.

Now, her grandmother and sister were presenting him with gifts. It was a good thing he'd thought ahead and ordered gift cards online when he'd been picking out the gifts for the children. When he'd entered the hallway to get Wendy and Morgan for their grandmother, he'd gone into the closet to reach into his coat pocket, where he'd slipped the envelopes with the gift cards inside.

"I don't know what to say," Gray said as he was tearing open the box.

When he lifted the top and pulled back the tissue paper he was shocked to see the gift was a newspaper article in a nice oak picture frame. The title of the article was The Taylors of Temptation.

"I clipped that thirty years ago," Granny revealed. She was sitting in her recliner, legs crossed at the ankles, her long charcoal-gray-and-white skirt giving way to bright red slipper socks that she had pulled all the way up.

"Your parents were so proud when they brought all y'all babies home. And you know what? The town was proud, too," Granny told him. "There were so many news people here. Way more than there are now. Everybody wanted to see not only the first set of multiple births in Temptation, but the first African American sextuplets in this town. It was monumental."

Gray held the picture in his hand, staring down at his mother's and father's smiling faces. They were sitting on the top step of the porch of the house where they'd lived, six baby seats with little bundles of life inside each one. It was the happiness in his parents' eyes that grabbed on to him and held tight. Gray never remembered seeing that look on either of their faces when he was growing up.

"Wow, you kept that all this time," Wendy said.

"I sure did," Granny continued. "That's what pride is. You believe in something forever and you stand by it."

"It's a wonderful gift," Gray said to her finally. "I really appreciate it."

Granny leaned forward, the recliner snapping upward with her motion. She didn't miss a beat, but rested one elbow on her knee and pointed a finger from the other hand at him.

"I don't want you to appreciate me giving you that picture. I want you to do something with your legacy. It's your duty and your parents expected it. They worked hard, saved and borrowed money to make it possible for the six of you to be here on this earth. It's shameful that none of you live in this town, or even bother to visit. I don't care how Olivia and Theodor's relationship ended, there was once love between them and you children are the product of that. Don't let it be in vain, you hear me? Don't disappoint them like that."

Once more Ida Mae Bonet's words echoed in Gray's mind, long after she'd spoken them. So much so that after the dinner at her house and after he'd dropped off Morgan and the children at their house, Gray returned to his room at the resort and called his sister.

"Merry Christmas," he said to Gemma the moment she answered.

"Well, merry Christmas to you, too, Grayson," his sister replied happily. "I thought you were going to be the only one I didn't speak to today."

"You talked to Garrek?" Gray asked.

"I sure did. Only for a minute, though, because he said something about needing to catch a flight, but it was good to hear his voice," she told him.

Gray nodded. "It's good to hear your voice."

She was quiet for a moment.

"Are you all right, Gray? Did something happen?"

He sighed heavily, rubbing his eyes as he'd also allowed himself to really think about what had happened last night.

"The community center burned down last night," he told her. "It's completely destroyed."

"Oh, no. How did that happen?" Gemma asked him.

Gray shook his head, then remembered he was on the phone with his sister and not having a face-to-face conversation with her. How long had it been since that had happened?

"Oh, no, Gray. That's such a shame. What's going to happen now?" she asked after a few moments of silence.

Gray sat back in the chair, the phone to his ear, his other hand pushing the curtains back so he could see out the small window in his room. He liked the view out of Morgan's bedroom window better because George was still standing, even though his bottom layer was partially melted, and his nose and one of his eyes were gone. It had snowed twice since the big storm, but there hadn't been much in the way of accumulation.

"I'm going to build a new one," he said simply.

The decision had been just that, simple and unquestionable.

"The town needs the community center and the hospital and we need to keep the house. It's what Mom and Dad would have wanted," he said for the first time out loud.

Gemma went quiet.

"Are you sure?" she asked finally.

Gray nodded again. "I'm positive. So listen, there's something else going on here. I went through Dad's papers and things and he left an envelope for each of us. I'm going to send them out tomorrow, so you'll have yours by the end of the week. He was doing some things that we didn't know and I'm still trying to figure them all out. But I've decided to keep all the buildings and see some of his intentions to fruition. I typed up a memo with a summary for all of you to look over, but I really think it would be a good idea if you all came to Temptation. Just to see how you feel about everything."

This idea had come to Gray while he sat at the cherry oak table in Ida Mae's house earlier that night. There was talk about the Valentine's Day dance coming up and then the Spring Fling, which they were all hoping that Millie did not plan the way she had last year. The children were excited about summer break and going swimming at the lake. All things that he and his siblings had done at one time in this town.

"Wait a minute, are you asking us to move to Temptation?" Gemma asked him.

"No," he replied quickly. "Not at all. I'm just thinking that we all owe it to Mom and Dad to do more. They cared about this place and since we were born here, maybe we should, too."

"Gray," Gemma said, "is there someone in that place that you care about now?"

He pinched the bridge of his nose. He had felt as if he had no one to talk to about all these new emotions brewing inside of him.

"She's a single mother. Multibirth, just like Mom. She teaches and she directs children's plays. No bigger than a fairy, but stubborn and resilient as hell. And the kids, they're adorable. Jack has a quick mind while Lily is the thinker—she contemplates and then decides. She's as sweet as candy, but serious and no-nonsense like her mother," he said before sighing heavily. "What am I going to do without them when I head back to Miami?" he asked, more to himself than his sister.

"Hmm, maybe you should be asking yourself what you want to do with them there in Temptation" was Gemma's reply.

Chapter 15

"Arson," Dave said solemnly as he sat across from Gray at Pearl's Diner, three days after Christmas.

"Used paint thinner and lots of it," he continued. "Started with it down in the basement, right near that fuse box you were talking about, and poured it all the way up to the top floor. The origin was in the basement, though, right by the back door, so they could escape quickly."

Gray rubbed a hand over his chin as he took in each word that Dave had said.

"Burned quick and fast, it did. Still hot over there, too, so don't you go poking around. I'll have a written report by the end of the day so you can send that to your insurance company," he told Gray.

"Thanks for that," Gray said. He'd just finished eating the best tuna and lettuce on whole wheat he'd ever had in his life and now he had to attempt to digest this news on top of that.

Dave shrugged and finished his coffee. "Just doing my job, nothing special."

"Would contacting the sheriff about your findings be part of your job?" Gray asked.

Dave nodded. "Sure would. And I've already done it. Sheriff Duncan and his deputy, Harlow, are going to meet me there in about an hour and I'm going to show them where I found everything."

"You mean the origin of the fire?"

"No. I mean where I found the earring and the bucket that points to who started the fire."

Gray sat straight up then, staring Dave directly in the eye.

"You know who set the fire?"

Dave Alderson was a stout man with an olive complexion, a center bald spot and bushy eyebrows. He wore a wedding ring on his chubby finger and a gold hoop earring in his left ear. Right now, he was rubbing that bald spot and staring at Gray as if he was torn between telling him the truth and waiting until someone else could take on that task.

"If you know, Dave, I want to know. I'd rather not wait until there's an arrest or the sheriff does whatever he's going to do. It was my building and I want to know," Gray told him.

"I don't have any obligations to tell you this. Hell, you ain't even a citizen of this town so I don't believe I owe you any allegiance," Dave told him.

Gray nodded his agreement to the man's words, all the while contemplating how it would look when he jacked him up by his collar and shook the admission out of him.

Dave leaned back against the seat and let his hands drop to the table. "But my mother was a good friend of your mother's, back when she lived here. I was about six and I can remember them two sitting on our back porch talking while I played with my dog, Loppy. Best damn golden retriever you'd ever want to meet. When he died it almost killed me."

Dave waved a hand as if telling himself to stop his speech. "Anyway, your mother had a kind smile and always gave me lollipops."

Gray didn't move a muscle, simply looked at the man expectantly.

"There was an earring left at the scene, just a few feet away from the back door. Got a little charcoaled but near as I can tell it's real gold, got some diamonds on the side of it, too."

"So the person who set the fire was a woman," Gray said, trying to connect Dave's imaginary dots.

"There was also a glove and a bucket," Dave continued. "The bucket was farther away—somebody dropped it behind the bushes down at the end of the block in the back of the building. It wasn't burned at all and it had a price sticker on the bottom of it."

"I don't know where you're going with any of this," Gray admitted, his patience with Dave growing very thin.

"Your little assistant friend, she was there getting sassy with Morgan and you that night," Dave told him. "She was only wearing one earring."

Gray frowned. "Kym? You think Kym did this?"

Dave shook his head. "Not by herself. You see that price sticker on the bucket—it's from Harry's Hardware down on Sycamore Street. The glove's a big one, large or extra large, I suspect for someone with big hands. Harry used to wrestle when he was back in high school. Was good at it, too."

The waitress came over then and Dave ordered another coffee. "Now, what do you think about that?" he asked Gray when they were alone again.

Gray sighed. "I have no idea what I think about everything you've just told me. None, except if we can prove this, I want their asses in jail for a very long time!"

"You're not supposed to be here," Sheriff Kevin Duncan said when Morgan walked up the path toward the stairwell leading to Harry's apartment.

Kevin was a fourth-generation officer in Temptation, having just taken over from his father in the last four years. He was taller than his father had been at just about six feet, with close-cropped hair and a full beard. His second-in-command was Harlow Biggins, who was the complete opposite of Kevin, with his short, round build, pale skin and scraggly stubble at his chin.

"It's a free country, Sheriff," Morgan said as she came to a stop right beside Gray.

She was spitting mad, had been since receiving Gray's call less than an hour ago.

"I just had lunch with the fire chief," he'd said solemnly over the phone.

Morgan had been cleaning up her living room, throwing away wrapping paper and boxes and those annoying plastic ties that came in the boxes with dolls and action heroes. She loved Christmas, but the days that followed always kept her moving as she tried to keep some semblance of order in a house where her kids could think about nothing but opening the next toy.

"What did he have to say?" she'd asked with the phone clutched between her ear and her shoulder, both hands full of trash that she stuffed into the recycle trash can.

"It was arson. Someone intentionally set the community center on fire. Well, not just *someone*." Gray had sighed then, but before Morgan could ask another question, he continued, "There's evidence to support that it may have been Harry and Kym."

"What? Are you serious?" she'd yelled so loud the kids

had actually stopped what they were doing to look at her. Morgan had made a conscious effort to calm the ripples of shock filtering through her at that moment.

"Tell me what's going on, Gray," she'd said in a slower, much more relaxed tone. A small smile had even crept along her face as she nodded toward the kids so that they could resume their play.

She'd listened to him talk, all the while walking back to her bedroom, where she slipped on her boots. "I told the sheriff that since I'm the building owner I wanted to be there when they questioned Harry," he'd informed her. "He didn't like it, but I didn't give a damn. We're headed there now."

"I'll meet you," she'd said in response before disconnecting the call. If he'd wanted to tell her not to come, it was pointless because she'd been in her car, dropping the kids off at Granny's in less than ten minutes, and now she was there.

"This is not how it works," Sheriff Duncan said, his brow furrowed as he stared at both Morgan and Gray. "My deputy is here to assist with this questioning. Civilians stay in their homes or at the station until I decide to brief them on what's going on."

"Except when it's my building that was burned to a crisp," Gray said sternly.

"And in my town, where some outsider and someone that I thought was a friend decided to burn that building to a crisp," Morgan added.

Harlow scratched the top of his head as he looked questioningly toward the sheriff. "You guys really think Harry could do something like this? He's lived here all his life. Hell, I used to play down at the lake with him and his sister when we were eight years old. His parents are as honest as they come."

"And paint thinner from his store was found at the scene," Gray said.

"Anybody could have bought that and left it there," Harlow quickly retorted. "Including that mean-spirited vixen that rolled into town behind you."

"And we're not going to know which one of them did it for sure if we keep standing out here freezing our butts off," Morgan added as she wasn't really in the mood for another male pissing match.

On the drive over she'd thought about her last interactions with Harry. The ones that included her trying her damnedest to keep Gray and Harry from coming to blows. No, the next time two men wanted to puff up and act like teenagers, she was going to let them. Especially since the memory of punching Kym in the face was still very fresh in her mind.

When the guys still stood there looking at one another she moved past them and headed for the steps. Harry lived in the upstairs apartment over top his hardware store. The entrance to his place was in the back and faced a thick copse of trees, with the lake running on the other side. She was just about to take the stairs when the sheriff grabbed her arm to stop her.

"I'll go in first," he told her, his grip on her arm light, but insistent.

Gray stepped up to him then, pushing the sheriff's hand away from Morgan's arm. "That's fine. We'll be right behind you."

The sheriff frowned and nodded toward Harlow. "Keep them at a distance while I do the talking," he said before walking up the stairs.

Harlow stayed behind Gray and Morgan, so close behind that when they'd come to a stop in a single-file line at the top of the landing, Harlow had bumped right into Gray's back.

Gray had stared at the deputy with irritation, while Harlow brushed down the front of his jacket as if it was somehow soiled at the connection. The sheriff shook his head in exasperation.

Knock. Knock. Knock.

Sheriff Duncan let his arm fall to his side and waited a few seconds.

"He's home," Harlow said from the end of their little convoy. "There's his truck over there."

Sure enough, Harry's older model beige 4x4 was parked at the end of the long grassy yard.

Knock. Knock. Knock!

They waited again, this time with the sheriff's frown growing almost as deep as Gray's.

"Open up, Harry Reed! I know you're in there. Don't make me call your momma over here with her key," the sheriff finally yelled.

A few seconds later the clicking of the locks could be heard and the door opened slowly. Harry peeked through the crack and said, "Yeah? What's up, Kevin?"

"This is official business, Harry," the sheriff told him. "I need to come inside and talk to you."

"Oh? What…" Harry began then looked around the sheriff to see Morgan and Gray standing there.

"What's going on?" Harry asked.

The sheriff sighed. "Let me in and I'll tell you what it's all about."

"No. I'm not letting all of you in my house," Harry insisted. "Especially not them, get the hell off my property!"

That order was directed to Morgan and Gray, of course.

"Don't mind them," the sheriff insisted. "The quicker we can get in and ask these questions, the quicker we'll be out of your hair. Is that smoke I smell, Harry?"

The sheriff was sniffing the air now, leaning in closer to Harry and the partially opened door. "You burning something in there?" he asked Harry, whose eyes had grown larger. "Let's just take a look."

Kevin Duncan was a lot stronger than his slim frame suggested. He'd gone into the marines right out of high school and had once entertained the idea of becoming an FBI agent. So he'd taken lots of classes at Quantico and still worked out feverishly to keep himself in shape. It was nothing to see him jogging through the streets of town in the early morning hours, or on the back porch of his house lifting weights.

Catching Harry off guard also made it easier for the sheriff to push his way inside Harry's home. Morgan followed him immediately, even while Harry cursed and swore to have some other authority come and throw her and Gray out. Harlow came bustling inside, positioning himself between Harry and Morgan and Gray, even going as far as holding a hand up at Gray to keep him from saying or doing anything untoward. Gray, of course, hadn't even acted as if that was what he was going to do. Instead, he held tight to Morgan's hand.

"Somebody's been in here smoking," the sheriff said as he looked down into an ashtray. "You don't smoke, Harry. Got company?"

Harry shook his head, his face angry and his hands fisted at his sides. "You got no right to be in here like this."

The sheriff nodded. "Okay, let me just ask you this straight out, then. Did you happen to sell somebody about a hundred gallons of paint thinner on Christmas Eve?"

Harry's lips trembled, his brow so furrowed it looked like all the excess skin from his head was rolled up there. "You got no right!" he yelled this time.

"Just answer the question, Harry. And then we can get going," Harlow insisted.

"Paint thinner is what caused that fire at the community

center," Kevin continued as he walked casually around the living and dining room area of Harry's open-concept place.

"A bucket of it was found behind the building. You know, after it burned to the ground," the sheriff continued.

"I don't have to say a word. I have rights," Harry insisted.

"You do," the sheriff said with a nod as he walked across the room, getting closer to one of two closed doors. "But I'll just keep on asking questions. Do you know a woman that would wear a diamond-and-gold earring? A big ol' hoop thing like the movie stars wear?"

Harry's gaze shot to Gray.

"I don't need you two here gloating. You got her all brainwashed and I lost. So what?"

"It doesn't have to be this way, Harry," Morgan told him.

She'd never seen him like this before. In fact, she wondered if this was even the same Harry she'd grown up with.

"Oh, yeah, it does. You made it that way. You went out and picked another outsider over me. He doesn't give a crap about this town or you! But that's for you to find out now. I'm done."

"So done that you burned down the community center?" the sheriff asked. "Did you have help or did you operate on your own?"

Harry looked over to the sheriff. "I want you to go now, too. You want something else from me, you get a warrant."

Harry moved toward the door, where Morgan guessed he was finally going to insist that they all leave without answering any questions. That's when she noticed he was only wearing his boxer shorts. Before Harry could say another word, another door opened. The sheriff stood expectantly as Morgan figured he'd just noticed Harry's state of dress, or rather undress, as well.

When Kym came through the door wearing leggings

and knee-length black leather boots, flipping her hair up from the inside of the sweater in a motion that told them she was just putting the garment on, there was total silence. Until Harry spoke.

"It was all her idea!" he blurted out. "She came here and stayed in my parents' place. Every night telling me about how her and Grayson were going to get married and make so much money. She said he was going to sell these buildings here and then they were going to elope. But that was all lies. That night she caught Gray and Morgan in bed together she was mad as a hellcat! Came banging on my door here saying I had to do something. That I needed to get Morgan away from Gray before something bad happened to her and the kids. So I proposed but you turned me down! You let that bastard toss me out of your place like he'd been the one to paint your kitchen and help plant that garden in the back.

"I was spittin' mad when I left your place and when I got back here she was sitting on my steps, legs crossed wearing those high heels that'll drive a man crazy," Harry continued. "She said she had the best way to take care of this once and for all. That the fire would wake Gray up and let him see that nothing in this town was worth his time and effort. He'd sell the other buildings real quick and head back to Miami. I didn't want to do it, my sister had her wedding reception at that community center. But I figured she knew Gray well enough that she'd know what his next step would be. She told me to go down to my store and get the paint thinner and then we waited until the play was over and everybody was out of the building. 'Cause I'd never hurt anyone. Not anyone in this town. We poured the thinner and—"

"Oh, for god's sake, shut up!" Kym yelled at him. "Don't

you know you have the right to remain silent, you dumb country idiot!"

"You are officially fired," Gray said to Kym through clenched teeth.

"Who gives a damn?" Kym spat. "I'm sick of this town and trying to convince you that the grass is definitely greener on the upscale side. You want to be here and play in the mud with them, have at it! I'm out of here."

She took a couple steps but was pulled back by the sheriff, who slapped handcuffs onto her wrists. "Not so fast, Ms. Upscale," he said to her. "You are under arrest for arson. You now officially have the right to remain silent."

"I'll let you get some clothes on first, Harry," Harlow said quietly. "Then I gotta arrest you, too."

"You did this!" Harry yelled at Morgan. "It was all your fault. We could have been happy, before he came here. You let him change everything, and for what? What's he promising you? Nothing, right? He's not offering to marry you, adopt your kids or even move here permanently." Harry shook his head. "It's all your fault!"

Harry kept talking even as Harlow ushered him into the bedroom to get his clothes. The sheriff walked out the door with a very angry, but now silent Kym, leaving Morgan and Gray alone.

"You do know that he's crazy," Gray said when Morgan had walked away from him to look out the window. "Nothing you or I did or said made them act the way they did. Absolutely nothing."

Morgan watched as the sheriff held a hand to the top of Kym's head as he lowered her into the back of his cruiser.

"I know that," Morgan said and then turned back to face Gray. "But what I don't know, Gray, is if everything that Harry and Kym said was totally wrong."

She didn't know what Gray's plans were in regard to

her and her family. She had no idea if his decision to keep the buildings in Temptation meant he wanted to keep her and the twins as well. Sure, she could simply ask the question, but right at this moment, Morgan wasn't so sure she wanted to know the answer.

Chapter 16

Second week of January

"I think this has run its course," Morgan said on a Friday evening when Gray had returned to Temptation.

The morning after Kym and Harry had been arrested, Gray had told her he needed to go back to Miami.

"I left a lot of things in limbo when I came here a month ago and I need to get back to my office. Especially now that Kym's gone. I'll need to see my attorney to confirm that all those ties are severed and I need to also work on obtaining legal ownership of the LLC account in the Grand Caymans," he'd said as he stood outside her house.

He'd called her and asked her to come out, to avoid seeing the children, Morgan had assumed. It was very early and since they were still on Christmas vacation, the children had been still asleep, so there was really no need for them to meet outside like sneaky teenagers. But Morgan hadn't bothered to say that.

"I understand," she'd replied instead.

"An architect and construction manager will be here by the end of the week. I want the new community center up and running by the spring," he'd continued.

"That's a good idea," Morgan had said.

"The hospital's renovations and new programs are going to take a little more planning. But I'll hire someone to spearhead that as soon as I get back to Miami," he'd said.

His hands were in the pockets of his leather jacket. He wore black wingtips, the cuff of his navy blue pants falling perfectly over them. Gray was wearing a suit again. He was officially *the* Grayson Taylor once more.

"I'm sure everything will work out just the way your father had planned," she'd told him.

"I'll call you" was the last thing Gray had said to her.

Morgan had only nodded because she hadn't believed him for one minute. And she'd been right to not believe him.

In the ten days that he'd been gone Morgan had not received one call. After the second day she'd stopped checking. Now, she was convinced it had all been for the best.

"Why don't we sit down and talk about this," Gray said.

Today, he wore his puffy coat and khakis. On his feet were black boots. His goatee had grown a little thicker, his complexion looked a little healthier. Or maybe that was simply because she hadn't seen him in a while. She didn't know, nor did she allow herself to care—too much.

Reluctantly, she let him into her house and walked to the dining room, where she sat at the table. Tonight was Disney movie night and since the community center was gone, the church board had approved hosting this monthly event in their fellowship hall. Granny had taken the twins, telling Morgan—in that not so polite but honest way that only Granny possessed—that Morgan looked like she needed some rest.

"There are some things I want to tell you," he began once he removed his coat and sat down. "Things that it has taken me some time to get a grip on myself."

Morgan immediately shook her head. "I'm not sure that's necessary, Gray. And really, it's not a big deal. We're both adults and we knew all the facts before walking into this…um, affair," she said and then had to clear her throat.

Morgan had never had an affair before and while this one had been fun while it lasted, she was positive that she never wanted to experience another one.

"Really?" he asked as he sat back in the chair, letting one arm rest on the table. "Why don't you tell me what those facts are."

This entire conversation was pointless. They'd slept together a handful of times, had dinner at the diner and played in the snow. Her kids adored him, but they were young and would soon find something else to fall in love with. He'd been gone for ten days with no communication whatsoever and now he was back looking as handsome as ever, but still not as if he belonged here. There was no changing any of that.

"Temptation is a small town, Gray. There are no highrise buildings, no nightclubs or fancy garages to park your equally fancy car. We're simple people here, living a simple life. I've never seen as many numbers on a bank statement as I did on that one that belonged to your father. And I do just fine buying my children's Christmas presents, but this living room has never been so full of gifts that I had to make a path to walk around them."

He nodded.

"And what exactly does all of that mean?"

He was eerily calm as he continued to study her. Morgan figured that may have been the way he studied a new car or a new pair of shoes before he purchased them, but no, his eyes were much too intense for that.

She sighed heavily. "It means that we were a mixed match from the beginning. I'm a widowed teacher with two children. You're an internationally known businessman with your own life and goals that I could never begin to compete with." She shrugged. "We were doomed from the start."

Gray rubbed a hand over his chin as he continued to look at her. Then he reached into his pocket and pulled out a red pouch. He set it on the table and they both stared at it for a few moments. He finally pulled the drawstrings and opened the pouch, pulling out a ring and sitting it on top of velour fabric. Morgan resisted the urge to gasp, but couldn't stop staring down at the huge sapphire ring with a circle of diamonds surrounding it. This looked just like the sapphire necklace he'd given her for Christmas, the one that she still had in a box in her underwear drawer.

"Along with the account my father had in each of his children's names, there was a safe-deposit box. This was in mine," Gray told her. "He was going to give this to my mother for her birthday. It was three months after their wedding anniversary when he planned to give her the necklace. Those dates were nine months from the day he walked out on his family."

Gray took a deep breath and then let it out slowly. He looked over to Morgan, his gaze softer now. "He never stopped loving her or us. I figured that out once I went through everything that was in his house, the pictures he kept, all the gifts my mother had ever given him, our first toys. None of that stuff was dusty or uncared for because he kept them out, he took care of them. Just as he always planned to take care of us. I have to believe that there was another reason for them breaking up, a reason that neither of them ever spoke of. If it was just an affair, why keep all those memories of the past?"

With his fingers, Gray brushed down his goatee, closing his eyes for a few moments before opening them again. "In the last weeks I've learned that life is not always what it seems, Morgan, and that sometimes people aren't, either. I thought I knew what I wanted and where I wanted to be, but I was wrong. The moment I left Temptation for the second time I realized that I wanted to be here with you and the children. But we're apparently too mixed matched for that."

She should have felt like a jerk for the things she'd said to him, but Morgan could feel only sorrow.

"Neither of us knew the things we know now when we first met," she said instead. "I've heard everything you've said about your parents and I'm so happy that you're finding out things that you didn't know before. But Gray, that doesn't change the differences between us."

"The social differences that don't mean a damned thing. Is that what you're referring to?" he asked.

Morgan clasped her hands together. "After you left, all people in town could talk about was how shocked they were that Harry had gotten involved in this situation. They couldn't figure out why he would do such a thing when before you came to town Harry had seemed so happy. It was easy enough to accept Kym's involvement because they didn't know her and didn't care to. But then that left me. I became the connection between Harry and you, to the fire and to the Reeds' utter embarrassment that their son was going to jail. All of that rested on my shoulders."

"It shouldn't have and you know that."

She nodded. "I do. But if I'd never gone to visit that house with you, if I had just stayed in my lane and let you go about your business, then maybe Harry's life wouldn't be ruined and the Reeds' reputation wouldn't be in shambles. Maybe a woman who only did her job and fell in love with a handsome man wouldn't have found herself in what she thought was dire circumstances and wouldn't be facing prison time. We can't undo the past," she told him. "But it's probably smart if we start to think about other people besides ourselves when we start working toward the future."

Again, Gray was silent. He looked at her and then down at the ring. After a few moments he put the ring back into the pouch and stuffed it into the pocket of his suit jacket once more.

"You seem to know how you feel on this subject," he said as he stood up and grabbed his coat. "I'll leave you alone with that decision."

And that was that, Morgan thought, as she got up from her seat and walked Gray to the door. Not nearly as hard as she'd thought it would be and certainly not as exhausting as the scene with Harry. Except, she spoke too soon.

When Morgan opened the door to let Gray out the twins came rushing inside.

"Mr. Gray! Mr. Gray!" they yelled in unison, both of them wrapping their arms around each of Gray's legs to hug him.

Morgan felt like a weight had been dropped on her chest as she watched Gray go to his knees to hug them both.

"You went away and we missed you!" Lily told him as she kissed his cheek.

"Yeah. I didn't have anybody to play with my train with me. Mom and Lily are girls and they don't understand," Jack complained when he kept an arm around Gray's neck and leaned in to him.

"I'll have to come around and play with you some other time," Gray told him. "Right now, I've got to go."

"No," Lily pleaded, her little face crumbling instantly. "Don't go away again, Mr. Gray. Please don't."

"We want you to stay here with us," Jack said. "We even wished on the mistletoe like Mama does."

"Right," Lily continued. "We wished for you to be our new daddy since our other one died."

Morgan swallowed and tried desperately to keep her composure. In the days that Gray had been gone the children had asked about him every day and Morgan had given them a very generic he-had-to-go-back-to-his-home reply. She'd hoped that in time the questions would stop, but apparently her children were missing him much more than she initially thought. Her stomach churned and she thought she might actually cry or faint, one or the other, or possibly both.

"There's magic in those wishes," Granny said.

Morgan hadn't even noticed her grandmother come into her house and take off her coat, but Granny was now standing right beside her.

"I'll be back," Gray told them. "I promise I'll come back and play with you sometime. And Lily, we can have another tea party."

Lily's bottom lip quivered, while Jack's remained poked out as Gray stood. He looked at Granny. "Nice seeing you again, Ms. Ida Mae."

"Good to have you back, Grayson," Granny replied.

Gray nodded and then looked at Morgan. He didn't say anything but turned to walk out of the house.

The moment the door was closed Morgan held up a hand to stop whatever words were about to come out of the mouths of her grandmother and her children. "Not right now," she told them. "Just, not right now."

She ran from the room at that moment, emotions swirling quickly and potently throughout her body, causing her to be sick.

Three days later Morgan lay facedown on her bed when Wendy came into the bedroom.

"Well, you missed a very lively MLK Day parade. Millie tried to ride one of the Coolridge horses instead of getting in the car with Mayor Pullum. You know she hates that woman with a passion."

Wendy talked as she moved around the room, pushed open the curtains, and then plopped down on the bed as she took off her boots and dropped them to the floor.

"Then Fred ran over to try and help her up, but the horse bucked and when it came down it was in a puddle of muddy water that splattered all over Millie's snow-white suit and Fred's suede jacket. And that's not all," Wendy continued. "Jerline Bertrum ate three huge bags of Mr. Edison's rainbow sherbet cotton candy and when it came time for her solo she barfed over the microphone and a good portion of the flower-lined float she was riding on. The kids all tried to laugh at first, but then there was a gust of wind and the smell hit everyone. There was barfing and crying and screaming. Girl, it was a mess."

Morgan groaned.

"You been laying here the entire time?" Wendy asked.

Morgan opened one eye to see her sister looking down at her. "Uh-huh," she murmured.

"Why? Are you sick?" Wendy flattened her palm on Morgan's forehead. "You're clammy but not feverish. You think it's the flu?"

"No," Morgan said quietly.

"Maybe it's that stomach virus that's been going around. Have you been vomiting or having diarrhea?"

Morgan did not want to think about either, but she was pretty sure she didn't have a stomach virus.

"I'm pregnant," she said, maybe even more quietly than she had the previous answer.

Wendy waited a beat and then said, "Excuse me?"

With a heavy sigh Morgan turned over onto her back, tossing the white stick she'd been holding in her hand for the last hour at her sister.

"What? Oh. My. Oh. My," Wendy said over and over again. "You're pregnant!"

"Give that girl a prize," Morgan sighed.

"It's Gray's baby. You're pregnant by Grayson Taylor," Wendy said as she bounced up and down as if it was the happiest day in her life. "Oh, just wait until Granny hears this. She's been talking about you and Gray for days now, saying how that mistletoe wish was bound to come true for the twins, no matter how you tried to stop it."

Morgan dropped an arm over her face and groaned. "I didn't try to stop it. I wanted to protect me and my kids."

"Whatever," Wendy said, thankfully getting up off the bed.

Morgan's stomach was not on solid ground, hadn't been for days now.

"There's no protecting people from falling in love. I don't know why anyone ever tries that stunt in the first place. And those children, they're too young to know about games and hiding from their feelings. They knew what they wanted all along," Wendy said.

"But he wasn't theirs to want," Morgan argued. "He wasn't mine. He didn't even want to be here."

"Well, he's certainly here now," Wendy told her.

Morgan sat up on the bed to see her sister with her cell phone in hand. "What do you mean he's here now? And who are you texting?"

"I'm telling Granny. You know she doesn't carry that phone around that we got her so I'm guessing it'll take her about an hour before she sees it. That gives you more than enough time to shower and pretty yourself up so you can go and tell Gray about the baby."

Morgan narrowed her eyes at her sister. "What? Wait. I don't know if we should be telling Granny yet. And it's my news so I should really be the one to tell her. And how am I going to go and tell Gray anything? He's back in Miami."

Wendy shook her head. "Nope. He never left Temptation. He's been staying at his parents' house. The one where construction trucks have been parked out front since yesterday. He's got work going on at the community center, the hospital and the Taylor house. So you can just go on over there and tell that man you're having his baby."

"I can't," Morgan said as she remembered all the things she'd said to him just days ago. All the things that she'd thought at the time were the right thing to say.

"You can and you will," Wendy said, now finished with her text message. She came over and grabbed Morgan by the hand.

"Stop thinking of reasons not to do it and just go. You can't keep his baby from him and you're certainly not the type to even consider any other option," Wendy continued.

"He probably thinks I'm some idiotic fluff head," Morgan complained as she entered the bathroom.

"Well, you've certainly been acting like one. But we can easily blame that on the pregnancy. Now, here, I'll run your water and when you get out I want you to put on the clothes I pick out for you. No fussing. Just get dressed and go," her sister ordered her.

"Wendy," Morgan said when she was standing near the shower stall, the water that her sister had turned on already sprinkling her arm. "What if he tells me to go away?"

Wendy shook her head as she smiled at her sister. "If he wanted you to go away, Morgan, he would have never come back to Temptation."

Chapter 17

The red doors were gone.

That was the first thing Morgan noticed when she stepped out of her car and walked across the street toward the Taylor house on Peach Tree Lane. As Wendy had already told her there was a large dump truck and a smaller white pickup parked on the front lawn. The dilapidated white picket fence that surrounded the entire corner property was gone and there were workmen moving in and out of the house.

"Is Mr. Taylor here?" Morgan asked one of the men as she stepped gingerly onto the front porch.

"Straight back, in the kitchen with the site manager," he said, barely looking at her while ripping another long slab of wood from the railing.

She walked into the house, seeing even more activity. There were holes in some of the walls, electrical wiring pulled out, several men standing around it talking about what they saw, she guessed. All the drapes had been removed from the windows and rugs had been taken up from the scuffed wood floors. Dust tickled her nose as she continued toward the back of the house. Nobody even asked why she was there—they all simply continued to work as if they didn't see her in the midst of their workday.

She stepped into the kitchen to see even more people, including Gray. He was standing in a corner, a bank of huge windows that went from one side of the wall to halfway around the other. The view of the backyard was stunning, but it was the tiny peak of the mountaintop that had Morgan moving closer without speaking a word. This was a gorgeous view and as she stared out to the cloudy January day, she had a quick flash of children playing in this yard. First, it was of multiple children, six to be exact, three boys and three girls, running and laughing, tossing a bright red ball between them. In an instant the scene remained the same, but the children were different—there were two of them, a boy and a girl. The red ball still rolled around the yard, with laughter and cheering loud in the air. On the porch, just a short distance away, was a cradle with a baby wrapped tightly in a blanket inside.

"Good afternoon," he said from directly behind her, his voice deep and warm.

Morgan spun around quickly, her back hitting against the windows as she faced Gray. He looked even better than he had a few days ago, she thought as she swallowed, trying to calm her jittering stomach. This wasn't morning sickness, although Morgan had been having her time with that. Hence the reason she'd finally purchased the pregnancy test.

"Hi," she said, her hands behind her, clasping the windowsill.

They were silent the next few minutes, both of them looking at each other as if searching for the right words to say. He wore a long-sleeved shirt today that melded against every muscle of his upper body. His jeans were dark denim, his boots black. If she didn't know better Morgan might have mistaken him for one of the crew. But she did know better. She knew that there was a three-inch scar under his right knee where he'd fallen off his bike and into a ditch when he was thirteen. She also knew that his favorite ice cream was chocolate and that he'd never been to Walt Disney World. Another thing she knew, without a doubt, in that instant that she saw him standing in this old kitchen where his family once lived was that she loved this man.

"I thought you were leaving," she said.

"I left your house because you told me to go," he replied, stuffing his hands into his front pockets.

Morgan nodded. "I know."

She'd told him that because she was afraid of hearing him say he didn't want to stay. It had all boiled down to that. Well, whether or not Gray stayed in Temptation he deserved to know that she was carrying his child. Regardless of how she felt about him—even though she'd been too silly and too cowardly to just tell him that she loved him—he was free to go wherever he pleased. She wasn't going to try and guilt him into staying with her. She was already a single mother, there was no reason why she couldn't continue on that way. After all, thousands of women did every day.

Morgan took a deep breath and decided it was simply best to say it and get it over with.

"I'm pregnant."

The words fell into the room that was bustling with activity around them. Still, they had the impact of a gigantic pink elephant stepping immediately between them.

One of his brows arched and Gray opened his mouth to speak. He closed it and then tried again. Nothing.

"Just about six weeks," Morgan continued. "So it must

have been that first time. When we were at my place. Um, I counted back and that had to be the night. I haven't been with anyone since James died, so I'm positive it's yours. I wouldn't be standing here if I wasn't absolutely certain."

She began shaking her head as he continued to stare at her. "But you don't have to do anything. I'll be all right. I mean, we'll be all right. I totally understand that you have a life in Miami and business and all that."

He slowly placed a finger to her lips. "Shush."

Morgan's heart was beating so fast that, coupled with the noise of something that had fallen in the other room, she had to ask, "What did you just say?"

Gray took a step closer to her. "I said to shush."

This time it was Morgan who opened her mouth to speak, just to have the words cut short when Gray grabbed her at the waist, pulled her up against him and kissed her.

It was what great chick flicks were made of. The slow and poignant hold, his gaze trained on her as he came in closer. Their lips parting slightly and then touching hotly. Morgan fell completely into the act the moment his tongue touched hers. She held him tightly, loving the feel of his strong arms doing the same to her. This was safe, she thought suddenly. It was safe and solid and…home.

"I thought you were leaving," she whispered against his lips when they'd had to choose between continuing the kiss or breathing. "I haven't seen or talked to you in weeks."

Gray shook his head. "I was giving you space," he told her and cupped her face in his hands.

"Space? I don't understand," she said, leaning into his touch, not wanting it to go away. "That day with Harry, you said if he truly loved me he would beg, steal, tear down walls and climb mountains to keep me. But you just came over here and started doing…what are you doing exactly?"

He smiled. "I meant exactly what I said that day. When a man truly loves a woman he'll do anything to keep her. So when you told me that you wanted me to leave, even after I told you that I wanted to be here with you and the children, I did exactly that. I also moved into this house and starting mapping out the plan to our future. It starts with renovating."

"Renovations? Our future? Gray, I'm sorry. I don't know if it's the noise or the dust, or the flip-flopping of my stomach that's making me a bit nauseous, but I don't get what you're saying."

He kissed her lips quickly, letting one of his hands fall to cup her still-flat stomach. "I'm saying that I was just waiting for you to come to the conclusion I'd already reached. All my life I've wondered about my purpose and my place in this world. I didn't think it could be that I belonged in the same town where I started out, or that I could possibly want what my parents had, but I do. I want the home and the family. I want a wife and children that will run and play in this yard and grow up in this small crazy town."

Gray shook his head as if he couldn't believe his own words. "You're the one that I've been waiting for all this time, Morgan. You're the one that made me see what it was I truly wanted and love you so very much for being too stubborn to just let me come into this town with my business-as-usual attitude. I love you for being strong enough to walk away if I couldn't truly commit to you. And I love you for this," he said, looking down at his hand on her stomach. "So very much, Morgan. I just love you."

Her eyes were full of tears, her heart beating so fast she thought it could be seen through her shirt.

"You're the one I've wished for," Morgan said, blinking furiously to keep her tears from falling. "All those wishes under the mistletoe, for all those years. And then you showed up. It was you all along, Gray. I love you."

"We're going to be so great together," he told her. "You, me, Lily, Jack and this one." He patted her stomach then. "We're going to be a family. The new Taylors of Temptation."

* * * * *

Christmas in
Paradise

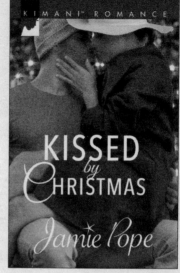

Jamie Pope

KISSED
by
CHRISTMAS

Hallie Roberts is ready to leave her big-city teaching job behind.
Then fate intervenes and brings gorgeous paramedic Asa Andersen
to her rescue. He makes it his mission to show her a romantic New
York Christmas. Can he convince Hallie to trust that their future is
worth every risk?

Tropical Destiny

Available December 2016!

HARLEQUIN®
www.Harlequin.com

REQUEST YOUR FREE BOOKS!

2 FREE NOVELS
PLUS 2 *FREE GIFTS!*

KIMANI™
ROMANCE

Love's ultimate destination!